THE ROKER'S REEF AFFAIR

Roker's Reef is a small island off the west coast of the USA. A visitor from the mainland is David Firth, a rising young executive who plans to take a vacation on the Reef, and perhaps write a book. However, as soon as he meets the attractive divorcée Enid Porter he changes course and becomes more interested in her. Because suspicion is aroused that David Firth has come to the Reef to prepare the ground for a takeover by his firm, a hatchet-man is sent and tragedy erupts, leaving him with little but unhappy memories.

THE ROKER'S REEF AFFAIR

THE ROKER'S REEF AFFAIR

by

Michael Cronin

Dales Large Print Books
Long Preston, North Yorkshire,
BD23 4ND, England.

British Library Cataloguing in Publication Data.

Cronin, Michael
    The Roker's Reef affair.

    A catalogue record of this book is
    available from the British Library

    ISBN   978-1-84262-850-8 pbk

First published in Great Britain 1982 by Robert Hale Limited

Cover illustration © Simone Byrne by arrangement with
Arcangel Images

The moral right of the author has been asserted

Published in Large Print 2011 by arrangement with
Michael Cronin, care of Watson, Little Ltd.

Dales Large Print is an imprint of Library Magna Books Ltd.

Printed and bound in Great Britain by
T.J. (International) Ltd., Cornwall, PL28 8RW

PROLOGUE

As a holiday resort Roker's Reef had never been the success that the founding members of the Roker Development Syndicate had expected.

It had some natural advantages, of course. It was no more than ten miles off the west coast of the States, and during most of the year it had a healthy climate; there were a number of attractive beaches where bathing was safe, and along the varied coastline there were attractive walks.

But it had no airport; throughout the season there was a daily ferry service from the mainland – it could be delayed or cancelled if the weather became too rough. There was a small harbour, and the beginnings of a marina; the sailing and the fishing were pretty good; there was no golf course yet, and only a few tennis courts.

Reef Town itself was more of an overgrown village than a town. The Reef Hotel was the best in the place, but it had little competition, and it was seldom more than a quarter full. There were the usual seaside boarding-houses, and a group of holiday cabins suitable for family occupation on a limited budget.

The Syndicate had originally planned to build a complete holiday complex, and they had taken over a controlling interest in the Reef Hotel and some other enterprises. But the holiday trade had never developed, and much of the planning had never got beyond the drawing-board.

At one optimistic stage a landing-strip had actually been hacked out of the countryside, and a holding surface rolled in as a runway. But it would take only light aircraft, with maybe two or three passengers, which was not much help where visitors in large and regular numbers were needed. Also, no air-line was prepared to take on such a footling little contract. It could never be made to pay.

So, after a short and expensive trial period, the strip had been abandoned, and it soon reverted to what it had been, a mess of scrub and tangled bushes.

There were too many established and well-publicised resorts up and down the coast, where the visitor could expect to arrive with the minimum of inconvenience in a jet just a few hours after leaving home.

If you wished for peace and seclusion and not too many outside distractions, then Roker's Reef might suit you, for a little while.

It was clearly no longer a place where a fortune might be made, and amongst those who had put their dollars into the Roker Development Syndicate there were now many who would be more than happy to get their money out again. There was no trading in the shares on any stock market, and none of the major share-holders visited the Reef any more.

Very soon it would be no more than an unimportant name on a map. Roker's Reef, where a few people still scratched a living.

ONE

Pat Quiney lived with his Aunt Emmie who kept a small grocery store down near the waterfront. Emmie was a widow, and she had been running the store for a number of years, just keeping afloat on a modest profit margin. Pat Quiney's mother had died when he was twelve, and Aunt Emmie had brought him up. His father, Mike Quiney, had been an indifferent provider ever since the death of his wife. He was a heavy surly man, with not many friends. For some years he had drifted from one job to another on the mainland, working on farms and saw-mills and docks.

For a time he sent money back regularly for Pat, and occasionally visited the Reef. There was even talk of taking Pat back with him one day soon, but the day never came. It is a bitter thing when a boy begins to realise that maybe his father is nothing special after all, that he is not to be really trusted because he doesn't do what he promises. And that you don't matter much to him. That happened to Pat by stages.

The remittances became smaller and less frequent, and nobody could mind that, because Mike Quiney was having some bad luck in his jobs. The visits stopped, and finally there was no contact at all with him. Pat wrote to the last address he had, a firm dealing in agriculture machinery in Nebraska, and after a couple of weeks the letter came back, the addressee had moved on and there was no forwarding address.

Aunt Emmie was Mike Quiney's sister, and she had no illusions about her brother. He was weak, and when the drink got the better of him as like as not he would fly into one of his black rages and it would take three or four strong men to handle him. That was how he was never able to hold on to a job for any length of time. He would be sorry afterwards, of course, but by then the damage would have been done ... and he would find himself in jail and out of work.

Aunt Emmie was a kind and understanding woman who did her best for Pat; he was the son she had never had, and on the whole the two of them got along very well. Pat helped in the store and around the house, and his absent father was now very seldom mentioned.

The Roker's Reef high school was small and poorly equipped, and attended only by the children of families who couldn't afford to send them over to the mainland as weekly boarders. Pat did just enough work to get by against little classroom competition, and he early showed an intelligent interest in mechanics and wood-work. Before he finished high school he had begun to work up a connection with the owners of motor-cruisers, and he could strip and diagnose the fault in a petrol or diesel engine much more efficiently than most mechanics on the Reef. Engines fascinated him, and any piece of machinery that wasn't doing what it was supposed to be doing was a challenge that had to be met and beaten.

In the back of his mind there was the notion that he would somehow get to college and qualify properly as a professional engineer. It would take money, so he kept the plan to himself. Aunt Emmie's store was making a smaller and smaller profit each season, since the Reef saw fewer and fewer visitors with money to spend. He was never going to take any more money from his aunt, he could earn it for himself, and in his last year at school he was already self-supporting, with money in the bank.

He had grown into a personable young man, with dark good looks, and plenty of charm when he chose to exert it. Social life at the level he could afford was limited on the Reef, and the entertainments at the hotels were out of his reach.

Most girls, particularly the good-looking ones, made him feel awkward and nervous. But he couldn't stop thinking about some of them, and the way the best ones looked in their bathing suits getting the sun on the deck of a cruiser, and pretty well showing all they had.

He did some odd jobs around the holiday cabins, running repairs and so on, mending windows and attending to simple plumbing bothers. It brought him into contact with some of the holiday folk, and he found a lot of them were friendly. In fact his first really complete sex experience had taken place in one of those cabins, with the able assistance of Mollie, a visitor whose husband was conveniently absent all the week on the mainland. Mollie was thin and too bony, and at first she scared him a little by her forthright approach to the matter of getting him into bed with her.

Before Mollie his erotic adventures had been meagre, some clumsy encounters that had left him unsatisfied and wondering what it was all supposed to be so wonderful for. It had never been worth the bother it took to get a girl into the mood when something might happen that he wanted and she pretended she didn't. Mollie altered all that in the space of one hot afternoon. She had his clothes off him in nothing flat – *my, what a build you got there, honey–*

She guided him over to the bed, and made him lie down. She wore very little, just a dress and pants, and she got out of those while he looked and wondered. It was the first time he had actually seen a naked woman. Not just the dirty pictures that got passed around the guys in the locker-room at high school. This was the real thing, it was strange and kind of dangerous, and he wanted her to stand still so that he could go on looking.

–what have you got there for me? Now let momma make you happy–

Mollie proceeded to do things to him that no woman had ever done before, accompanying her attentions with an obscene litany that he had never heard a woman use.

He had called on her to repair a piece of broken fencing, and when he left her that afternoon the fence was still broken. He was bemused and elevated. He had discovered the secret of living, and it had exhausted him, temporarily.

That evening he sat and drank beer in one of the waterfront pubs, something he seldom did because he had better uses for his money. His mind was filled with pictures of some of the saucy contortions Mollie had got up to on that bed. Fancy being married to a woman like her, she would drive a man nuts for sure.

Aunt Emmie guessed something had happened to him; he had that absent look about him, and he hadn't heard a word she had said to him all through supper. She was always hoping he would find a nice girl, there were some on the Reef, daughters of old friends of hers who would be suitable companions for Pat. When Aunt Emmie arranged to have any of the girls for tea on a Sunday, Pat would take little obvious interest in the girl, he would be just polite. He'd had a few girl-friends, Emmie knew that, but they had never lasted long.

One day soon Pat would leave the Reef, it had to happen, and Emmie knew she would miss him so much that she didn't care to think about it. He was her dear boy, and everyone said how handsome he was. There was nothing to keep him with her for much longer.

The next morning Pat set out for Mollie's abode of bliss, and Aunt Emmie had to remind him that he was supposed to spend the morning working on one of the motor-cruisers for Mr Olestead at the Reef Hotel.

'You promised you'd have it ready by to-night, Pat,' she said. 'Mr Olestead gives you plenty of work, so you mustn't let him down...'

'I'll see to it if I have time,' he said, and went off out, carrying his bag of carpenter's tools, which even Aunt Emmie knew would be of little use in fixing the engine of a motorboat that had ignition and other troubles. She also noticed that he was not heading down to the harbour, and she hoped he knew what he was doing because Charlie Olestead could turn real nasty when things didn't go right, and Pat couldn't afford to offend him.

He was getting headstrong, and he wasn't listening to her advice any more, he was growing up, that was what it was. There were flashes of his father's nasty temper showing up in him sometimes, and when that happened it was better to leave him alone.

When Pat reached Mollie's cabin he knocked at the door; he knew he was being watched by the woman in the neighbouring place, and there were two kids out in the front garden, also watching him. When Mollie didn't answer the door, he took a quick look at the railing he should have mended yesterday. It was a simple job and it wouldn't take long. It was just possible that Mollie might be sleeping late, and from what he remembered of her place she didn't go much on house work, not like Aunt Emmie who kept their little house spotless and ran her store as well.

15

So he clattered about, hammering and making workmanlike noises. The two kids from next door sidled closer to give him better attention. Pat ignored them, kids didn't interest him, and their mother was still there at her window, nosey bitch. So this visit to Mollie looked like being a public performance.

She had told him that he was the only one who had made love to her, apart from her husband. He wondered if she had been telling him the truth, he wanted to believe her, it made him feel better, sophisticated and no longer a youngster who didn't really know what it all amounted to. He knew now, hell, he knew all right.

He worked for well over an hour, and then he saw her pushing a bike up the short slope in front of the cabin; there was a basket strapped to the rear carrier of the bike; Mollie wore tight green shorts for which she didn't have the legs, and a coloured tee-shirt.

'Hi,' she called, 'just remembered a bit of shopping, okay?'

There was a loud maternal summons from the place next door, and the two kids scampered in and out of sight.

Mollie laughed. 'Maybe I've become the scarlet woman around here all of a sudden. You finish the job, Pat, and I'll see if I can rustle up some refreshment.'

She took her basket indoors, and Pat went

on with his labour very conscientiously for another half an hour, and whenever he glanced across he caught a glimpse of the woman next door who was keeping an eye on him. He was tempted to give her a rude signal. He knew who she was, Mrs Alice Tarrant, her husband Tommy was with a construction gang that operated along the coast on the mainland. Tommy was okay, a good man with a concrete-pouring job, and the rumour was that he couldn't stand his Alice for long, which made sense to most men who knew both of them. And that included Pat.

Mollie opened her door. 'Finish in five minutes,' she said, and left the door open.

Pat finished off tidily, even sweeping up afterwards. Then he went in and put his bag of tools just inside the door.

'Food first, like the sailor said.' There was coffee and a plate of sandwiches, rather thick and inelegant sandwiches, corned beef and pickles.

'That old bird next door, Alice Tarrant, is she likely to talk?' said Pat. 'It doesn't bother me, I was thinking of you–'

'You scared of my husband?' she asked. 'You needn't be, we have one of these open-ended marriages – I know my Jimmie, and I know he isn't sleeping on his own all through the week. Most week-ends when he comes back he's too tired to raise a gallop.

So I do what I want to do, and if Mrs Alice Goddam Tarrant doesn't like it she can take a running jump, now eat that chow because my patience is getting exhausted.'

Pat thought this was an ideal set-up – sex on tap and with a woman who knew the whole of the score. She let him finish the sandwiches. The sink in the kitchen was loaded with dirty crockery, but Mollie did nothing about them, the kitchen was not her favourite working arena.

When Pat had satisfied one of his healthy appetites he followed her into the bedroom. It was little more than midday on a bright sunny day, and Mollie ostentatiously drew the curtains together, so that Alice Tarrant would know for sure what was about to happen with the loose woman and the young lad.

If she had been a spectator in the room a few minutes later she might have found the goings-on scandalous – and regretfully well outside her limited experience.

At one stage when they were momentarily at rest, Mollie remarked, 'I'm your first, aren't I? You never really had anything to do with a woman before, not properly, like this, did you?'

'No, hell no … nothing like this ever before…'

'I ought to be charging you for this, part of your education – the important part that counts.' She giggled. 'I must admit you're a quick learner–'

'And you're a pretty smart teacher.'

'You have a good body,' she said. 'A couple of years from now you'll be one hell of a lover, you have the apparatus and you like it, you'll always find some woman who'll put out for you.'

'You're all I want,' he said, and believed it himself for the time being.

'You're kidding me,' she said gently, 'but it's nice of you to say that. I don't think you're going to forget me in a hurry.'

'I couldn't,' he said. 'But you talk as though we were finishing, and we've only just begun.'

'I want you to come and spend the night with me, tomorrow night. Can you do that?'

He got himself up on one elbow and looked down at her, and she smiled up at him and said, 'Wouldn't you like that?'

'I would, you bet I would!' he said with a load of enthusiasm.

'It's the only way to get the best out of making love,' she said, 'to be together all night long, no hurrying, no fussing – you've never made love in the early morning, there's nothing like it. Now I'll have to ask you to be a good boy and leave me, I have some folk coming in and I have to clean the place – they're women, so you needn't look suspicious. We have a firm date for tomorrow night, okay?'

'Okay,' said Pat. 'I wish I could stay longer...'

'Save it for tomorrow,' she said. 'Round about ten, don't announce your arrival, just walk in, honey – I'll be here waiting. Now climb into your pants and scoot.'

Pat was happy to find Aunt Emmie in the store, so he was able to pick up his tool-box, the right one this time, and then he went down to the harbour. The motor-cruiser that he was due to work on was the *Sea Witch*, a flashy craft with lots of metal fittings and padded seats; the engine wasn't so hot, Pat had worked on it before.

He was about to start when Charlie Olestead came along the wooden walk, and he was looking anything but pleasant.

'What the hell kept you?' he snapped. 'You think I got nothing better to do than chase after you, boy? You should have finished that job by now, I promised a client it would be ready for him and you haven't even made a start!'

Pat looked up. It would have given him much pleasure to climb up there on the boardwalk and toss that loud-mouthed pig into the drink ... if he calls me boy just once more that's what I'll do...

They had an audience, some folks working on their boats nearby, all of them acquaintances of Pat's, including a couple of girls, and they were all beginning to show interest. Charlie Olestead liked having an audience when he was chewing somebody out, it showed he was the boss.

'You needn't expect any more work from me,' he went on, 'not unless you improve your attitude...'

'It'll be okay, Mister Olestead,' said Pat with a politeness he was far from feeling. 'I'll do a good job for you, I can promise you that.'

'You'd better,' said Olestead. 'Another mess-up like this and you'll be off my list for good, you hear?'

'Sure thing, Mister Olestead, don't you fret.'

'Don't you tell me what not to do,' said Olestead savagely. 'I'm here to give you instructions and I'm going to make pretty goddam sure you carry them out, you got that?'

'Sure thing.' Pat wasn't touching his forelock, but his whole demeanour was obsequious, and Charlie Olestead glared down at him, and wondered if this sassy layabout was trying to get a rise out of him.

So he pointed a commanding finger down at Pat, and said, 'As soon as you got it running, you report to me, right?'

'Yessir! You can rely on me!'

'So get on with it.' Olestead stamped back along the boardwalk, and Pat gave him the traditional two-fingered salute, and wished he would break both legs on the way.

Pat spent some hours working on the engine, but he could do no more than a patched-up job; the engine had been badly handled in the past and needed a complete overhaul, or even a replacement. He got it going and ran it around the harbour; it might run for some time, and then again it might pack up, as before. It was the best he could do.

He made out a work-sheet and a rough sort of account, and walked up to the Reef Hotel. He had padded his account to the tune of fifteen dollars, which he reckoned was pretty modest in the circumstances, and he didn't think he'd be getting much more work from fat Charlie in the forseeable future, the lousy bastard.

Charlie wasn't in his office and nobody seemed to know where he was. But Lucy the cashier was available and she had the authority to settle small local accounts. She thought Pat was a nice hard-working young man, a credit to his Aunt Emmie, with whom Lucy was on friendly terms. Thus Pat was able to collect his cash without any query.

'You can tell the old buzzard I did a nice quick job, same as he wanted – and I hope it sinks next time he takes it out.'

'Now Pat, that's no way to talk,' said Lucy. 'It's not nice...' But she was unable to hide a smile as Pat went out.

Since he very seldom spent a night away from home, he had to think up an alibi to cover the forthcoming all-night session with the gorgeous Mollie. As a school-kid he had spent the night sometimes at another kid's home after some party or other when it might be too late for him to get home. In recent years he was seldom away, just a few week-end trips across to Fairhaven. So he couldn't just waltz in and explain to dear old Emmie that he would be spending the night in bed with a married woman, and that he confidently expected this would be the first of many happy occasions of a similar nature.

Ossie Sinclair was his best bet to fix a fireproof story. Ossie helped his father to run a small farm right down on the south end of the Reef, near the coastguard station. Ossie was older than Pat and regularly had rather more spare cash, so that his area of operations was a lot wider and more varied than Pat's. He could get hold of a motor-cruiser sometimes when work on the farm was slack, and he could afford to spend time and money drinking in some of the mainland dives, and having carnal knowledge of any presentable female who happened to be available, although Pat occasionally suspected that Ossie was a bit of a liar about the number of women he could take care of in a boozy week-end.

The Sinclair farm was some five miles away, and Pat did not intend to walk; he collected his bicycle from the shed at the end of Emmie's little garden, and he managed to avoid letting Emmie see him, which was a fair start.

He reached the farm as Ossie was cleaning up after the milking. Old Sinclair was not in sight, and that was a bonus because he didn't like Ossie being interrupted when he was supposed to be busy on his farm chores.

Accordingly they adjourned to the feed store, which allowed Ossie a clear view of the house in case the old man appeared. Ossie had sandy hair and a wispy little bit of a beard of which he was very proud; he wore a tee-shirt and jeans stuffed into rubber boots, and he carried with him a pungent cow-shed aroma. He rolled himself a cigarette, while Pat outlined his problem, as one man of the world to another, leaving out Mollie's name and exact location.

'So you're dipping your wick tomorrow,' said Ossie thoughtfully, 'and all night, you hope.'

'That's putting it a bit crudely,' said Pat. 'What I need is a story that Auntie will swallow.'

'We mustn't hurt the old biddy's feelings,' Ossie agreed.

'I just want an excuse that sounds all right.

You're a good liar, Ossie, what can you suggest?'

'What a charming boy you are,' said Ossie. 'How about if I get my old man's car and call for you tomorrow evening on account of you are coming to a party with me? An all-night birthday party, for me? You can bring me a bottle of hooch as a present.'

'It might work,' said Pat.

'You tell it right and I'll be very surprised if it doesn't work. You're a grown boy, you're entitled to a night out now and then. Don't make it too fancy, just a party for a few of my old friends.'

'You're a pal,' said Pat.

'We'll have a few snorts maybe in the *Jolly Sailor,* just to get you in the mood, and then I'll drop you off so's you can get on with your foul plans for the rest of the night. If she's any good, Pat, I'll expect a detailed report in due course. She could be a bit of local talent that I've overlooked so far.'

'Are there any?' said Pat. 'I doubt it.'

At breakfast the next morning Pat announced that he had been invited to a birthday party at the Sinclair farm, and that it would probably go on all night. Aunt Emmie's concern was about his clothes, whether he had anything fit to wear to a birthday party. So he added the detail of a barn dance, for which a clean sports shirt and jeans would do all right, and everybody else would be wearing just that.

Aunt Emmie was aware that Ossie's reputation was a little unsavoury, but a party at the Sinclairs farm had to be all right, Mr and Mrs Sinclair would be there, and they would make sure there was no nonsense.

Fortunately for Pat, he had enough work to keep him occupied all day, but even so he couldn't stop himself thinking about what was going to happen that night. He wished he could afford to buy her a present, but he didn't see how he could possibly fetch up at her house with a bunch of flowers, for instance, and he didn't have the cash for buy anything better, like a brooch or something like that. Later, perhaps, because he was going to be seeing plenty of Mollie.

TWO

The first part of the evening went very smoothly. Ossie arrived in his father's car, and he looked tidy and respectable. He made the right kind of polite chat with Aunt Emmie, and with complete aplomb accepted her good wishes for his alleged birthday, together with a large box of chocolates as a present. With ponderous jocularity he promised to see that Pat didn't drink too much, and undertook to return him home in good condition some time in the morning.

Aunt Emmie hoped they would all have a nice time, and with all the sincerity of the practised liar that he was, Ossie assured her that they surely would, and they set off.

There were some hours to be got through before Pat could present himself at Mollie's door; she had said round about ten. The *Jolly Sailor* was Ossie's favourite watering-hole, and it was there that they were to pass a couple of hours. The interval there was to prove quite disastrous for Pat. He normally drank beer, and whisky was usually beyond his reach, whereas Ossie was a whisky-drinker with a reputation for rapid consumption, he also had the ability to remain in control of the situation when he should have been flat on his face on the floor.

After some quick rounds, Pat knew this pace was going to be too hot for him, and tried taking some food on board, but the *Jolly Sailor* had little to offer, beyond cold sausages and sandwiches and cheese; this was a place for dinking, if you wanted proper grub you could go along the street where they served it.

'Hey, boy,' said Ossie genially, 'you're not smashed already, the night is young and we got a long way to go.'

Pat was losing touch with his surroundings, and he was soon too fuddled to notice that no matter how much he tipped down his throat his glass was always full. The liquor loosened his tongue, and Ossie had no difficulty in ascertaining the identity of the lady who was scheduled to be spending the night with Pat. Mollie was not exactly a stranger to Ossie, he had never been with her, but he knew guys who had, and he reckoned she was going to be wasted on Pat – every time he lifted his glass he became more of a dead loss to a woman of Mollie's experience.

So Ossie kept the drinks coming up, and at this sloppy stage Pat was determined to show that he could hold his liquor as good as anybody there. They had by now become part of a school of drinkers, all matured and seasoned boozers, except Pat. He had broken into a sweat, and nothing would stay still around him. Very funny...

Ossie had to have help to get Pat out and into the car, where Pat made some sad grunting noises.

'You throw up in here, boy, and I'll wipe your face in it,' said Ossie, and he made sure the window on Pat's side was open. He kept a watchful eye on his passenger as he drove carefully out in the side road that would lead to Mollie's neighbourhood. Pat wasn't making a sound now, he had passed out, smelling like a distillery.

When he parked outside Mollie's place he switched his lights off; there were lights in some of the other cabins, but not in Mollie's, so he wondered if Pat had got it all wrong. Maybe Mollie wasn't there at all.

He gave Pat a vigorous shake, but it failed to rouse him, it just jiggled his head about. He was right out. Ossie went quietly up to Mollie's door and tapped, discreetly. There was no answer, so he knocked this time.

The door opened, the room was dark, and a voice inside there whispered something that sounded like an invitation to enter, which he did. He could smell her perfume, and he gently closed the door behind him, and said softly, 'I have Pat outside in my car, he's stoned, shall I bring him in?'

'Who the hell are you?' There was no female panic in Mollie's voice.

'Ossie Sinclair, from the farm over by the coastguard place—'

'Stay right where you are, don't you move a foot!'

There were some faint rustling sounds, and the light came on. Mollie wore a short wrap, bright red and yellow, one hand held it closed in front, and in her other hand she balanced a large copper jug. Her feet were bare, with scarlet toe-nail polish, and the rest of her that was immediately visible had been madeup for company.

'So what's this about Pat?' she demanded.

'I got him outside in my car,' said Ossie. 'We had a few drinks, and I guess he didn't know when he'd had enough, so now he's got no legs, if you see what I mean.'

'He's paralytic?' said Mollie.

'That's it,' said Ossie. 'I knew he was supposed to be coming here, so I brought him.'

'That's nice,' she said savagely. 'So everybody in the neighbourhood knows!'

'Only me,' said Ossie. 'Nobody saw me come here. Look...' He held out both hands, palms uppermost. 'Not a quiver,' he said. 'Pat can't hold whisky... I'm sober.'

'Good for you,' she said sarcastically. 'Do you think it's okay to dump him on me – you'd better have another think.'

Ossie put on a thoughtful look. 'Well, I thought it might be a good idea to let him sleep it off, in my car.'

'Outside my front door where they can all see him?' she said. 'You're full of bright ideas, you are.'

'I'll move the car,' said Ossie. 'There's plenty of cover in the bushes around here, and I turned my lights off before I stopped, so nobody saw me come here, and Pat'll be no bother, he won't know a thing until tomorrow morning, I guarantee that.'

'I don't think I'm with you,' said Mollie. 'What's on your mind?'

'I thought I might come back and visit with you,' said Ossie.

'Now I wonder what made you think that?' said Mollie softly. She put the copper jug on the table between them. 'Ossie Sinclair, I've seen you around the place. Pat told you he was coming here?'

'It sort of slipped out,' said Ossie. 'He got stoned pretty quick, and I came over here because I didn't want you wondering what had happened.'

He smiled at her, and there was nothing of the eager but slightly scared youngster about him. He was no Pat Quiney.

'You got your nerve,' she said, but not in the tone of an outraged lady who is about to toss an intruder out into the night. She inspected him quite openly. Maybe he didn't have Pat's muscles and build, but he knew what it was all about, and he was there on the spot and very ready to try his luck as a substitute. The thought of Pat drinking himself stupid while she was actually waiting here for him, that showed what an unreliable lover he was for a woman like her.

'So you expect to come back?' she said lightly.

'I bet you make a terrific cup of coffee,' he said.

'You'd better come back and try some. Wait until I put the light out, and you be quiet about it, you hear?'

'I hear,' he said. The light went out, and he crept out and down to where he had left his

31

car. Without putting his lights on he let the car roll silently down the slope that joined the service road. There was a small clearing further along where some timber had been stacked. He parked his car alongside. All the while Pat was snoring like some old bulldog, and he didn't smell so fragrant either.

Ossie collected the bottle of whisky he had conned Pat into buying for him at the *Jolly Sailor,* and he made sure the passenger's window was well down in case Pat woke up and had to spew, which was not unlikely.

He made a discreet entrance back into Mollie's place, and she waited until he had shut the door before she put the light on. She was wearing slippers now, with that brightly coloured wrap, and she was far from offended when she saw the whisky. She had the coffee ready.

'How was Pat?' she asked, pouring the coffee.

'Stinking,' said Ossie. 'A nice kid, when he's sober. I'll see he gets home, later, okay?'

'I'm not worried,' said Mollie. 'I wouldn't want you to think I do this kind of thing very often, you know what I mean?'

Ossie nodded profoundly. 'I know, anyone can see that you are a pretty special sort of woman.' From where he sat he could see into her bedroom. The light in there over the head of the bed was soft, and the bed was wide and inviting.

The coffee was fine, and now they had begun to work together on the bottle of whisky in a very friendly fashion, and with the mellowing of the atmosphere Mollie was becoming a little careless about the front of her wrap. She had nice firm breasts, and they were worth more than the fleeting glimpses Ossie was getting.

He was ready to pounce, but kept himself in check because when he went after a woman it had to be the real thing and no messing about. He continued to pour whisky into her at intervals, and slowly caressed the generous expanse of thigh that she was showing.

She put him off his stroke when she had a sudden giggling fit, followed by a noisily amorous assault when she tried to tug his shirt off and get his belt undone, as though she intended to rape him then and there on the creaking settee.

That was okay with Ossie, but it would be a hell of a sight better across there on that nice wide bed.

'Hey, baby,' he protested, 'let's go to bed and do this thing properly, okay?'

'Gimme some loving,' she mumbled, smearing slobbery kisses over his face. She had got rid of her wrap, and he was finding her a delightful load to handle.

'Take it easy, baby,' he said, 'let's not boil over...'

He got her to her feet and coaxed her across to the bedroom. He lowered her onto the bed and dodged her reaching hands as he got out of his clothes.

'You asked for it, now you're gonna get it...'

Her giggle became a high-pitched yelp when he took her. Ossie did not believe in finesse when he was in bed with a woman. Sex was a primitive encounter where the male had to dominate the female, and treat her as roughly as he thought fit. There was no affection or tenderness about the business. It was an urge that had to be satisfied, and in Ossie's limited experience plenty of the older women liked being roughed up as long as there was nothing to show afterwards, like a black eye or a busted nose.

Mollie protested at some of the more vigorous aspects of his attack.

'Hey, Ossie boy,' she said, 'you aiming to break me into little bits?'

'You know you like it,' he said.

'Give a girl a little space to breathe,' she pleaded.

He bit her neck. 'I'm putting my mark on you, baby,' he said.

'Now you're hurting me – ouch, Ossie! How about a little rest now? The night is long and we've only just started – you want to kill yourself?'

'I'm better than Pat, right?'

'No comparison, honest, Ossie – you don't have to prove anything any more.'

He allowed her a short respite, she had her head pillowed on his shoulder; she had a skinny figure, but that didn't seem to matter once she got active in bed, and she had those good knockers.

He had to visit the bathroom, and when he came back she lay on her side and she appeared to be asleep. He prowled around the room, he was always interested in a woman's bedroom, the really private bits. Mollie was a sloppy housekeeper, even her bedroom wasn't tidy. There were clothes scattered about and her dressing-table was a mess, spilt powder and stuff all over the glass top.

He rejoined her on the bed, and turned her onto her back. She did not come instantly alert and ready to co-operate again. It was like trying to make love to a dummy. And after a while he gave it up and let her go back to sleep.

It was a grey dawn breaking over the Reef when Ossie went quietly back down to his car. Pat was still inside. He roused himself when Ossie had the engine going. He looked very battered and bewildered and unhappy.

He held his head in both hands. 'What happened?' he whispered. 'God, I feel awful–'

'You look it,' said Ossie, 'boy, do you look a wreck. What happened? You got drunk and

I deputised for you, if you see what I mean?'

'You mean Mollie?'

'That's right, I don't reckon you should visit Mollie again too soon, if ever – she won't give you much of a welcome–'

'You bastard,' said Pat. 'You sneaked in there, you took a lousy advantage just because I had a few drinks too many – and you're supposed to be my pal! I ought to break your goddam dirty neck for that!'

Ossie stopped the car. 'If that's the way you feel you can walk home,' he said. 'You drank the whisky, so you can't blame anybody else – boy, you really do have a hangover, and you're not smelling too sweet either. What the hell, Pat, you fouled that up all right.'

Pat sat in the car and gazed sadly out over the countryside. There was an unpleasant mist spreading over the scene. 'Emmie will have the hide off me if she sees me like this,' he said. He glanced across at his smiling companion. 'What did Mollie say?'

'Nothing much. What could she say? You got stoned and left her dangling, so I moved in, and I didn't hear any complaints afterwards.' Ossie watched Pat twitch and get tensed up, just for a split second, and he quite expected that he would have to dodge a punch in the mouth.

Pat exhaled loudly. 'She must think I'm a dope,' he said.

'Could you blame her? Take my advice

and keep away from her, Pat.'

'Did she say she didn't want to see me again?'

Ossie got the car started. 'Why don't you grow up?' he said. 'The fact is that we didn't talk about you, not much. Why should we? I was there on her doorstep, and she was ready to be friendly. And that's all there was to it. To tell you the truth, I don't suppose I'll even call on her again. She's just another lay, Pat. Not a bad one, I'll give her that, but there's plenty of women who are good in bed, it's nothing all that special...'

Pat brooded over the situation. As he understood it, Mollie was ready to go to bed with any man who was available, who he was made no difference to her – he was just another body. Ossie was right – she was just another lay.

After Ossie dropped him he reached home through a back lane, and let himself into the back of the house, and he moved with the utmost care. Fortunately Emmie was a heavy sleeper. He made himself some coffee and took some aspirin tablets. In the bathroom mirror he looked at himself and he didn't much like what he saw. He looked the way he was feeling, depressed and deflated – and it was never going to happen to him again.

If Ossie spread the story around, life on the Reef wouldn't be worth living. So Pat made himself a solemn promise: he was going to work all the hours he could, he was going to take on any job that came his way, and he was going to save his money. When he had enough, he would go for the big move, across to the States, Europe maybe.

He had washed and changed his clothes and sharpened himself up by the time Emmie appeared, and she was pleased and surprised to find that he had made a start on getting breakfast.

'I didn't hear you come in,' she said. 'How was the party, Pat? Did you have a nice time?'

'Reasonable,' said Pat. 'We just had a few drinks and played a few discs, nothing too crazy.'

'Perhaps you're getting too old for birthday parties,' she said, smiling. 'Weren't there any nice girls there?'

'I didn't speak to a single girl all night,' said Pat, which was the simple truth.

'That sounds very dull,' Emmie said.

'It was,' said Pat.

For some months he stuck to his resolution to lead a hard-working life with no distractions in the shape of females. As a general handyman and a mechanic with a talent for fixing engines, he had little trouble in finding work. He had no overheads, he never minded how long a job took to complete, and he was ready to under-cut whatever competitors there were. He saw Mollie out shopping a couple of times, but he didn't speak to her and she didn't see him. Later he heard that she had moved back to the mainland.

There was one weekend when he went across to Fairhaven with Ossie Sinclair on what was supposed to be a bit of a party in one of the sporting houses Ossie knew about. This time Pat kept sober, but the woman he went with took little interest in the proceedings and charged him fifty dollars in advance.

He spent some weeks wondering if he'd picked up a dose, which Ossie thought was real goddam funny. It turned out okay.

He had a mild flirtation with a young music student who was convalescing after an operation. Mildred was stopping in one of the few guesthouses; it was run by a friend of Aunt Emmie's, which was how Pat came to meet Mildred. She was about his age, very slight, with auburn hair and a pale invalid colouring that made her appear even more fragile than she really was. When she smiled at him Pat reckoned she was really beautiful, sort of delicate, a girl who needed looking after.

She was not allowed much exercise at first, and they took short walks together in the evening, when the heat had eased off. Pat never touched her except perhaps to help her over some rough spot where the footing was uncertain. She talked to him a lot about herself and her life and the music she loved, and he didn't follow too much of the music talk. She was learning the piano, and she didn't go in for pop, just the classical stuff, Beethoven and Mozart, and that lot.

He liked listening to her, and looking at her. She wore slacks sometimes, but when she wore a skirt she didn't mind him admiring her legs when he helped her over a bit of rock. To him she was a new sort of girl, the kind a guy might think of marrying one day.

When she went home to Cedar City they wrote to each other for a while, and made some long-term plans to meet again. The reunion never happened, and gradually the letters stopped.

Aunt Emmie was sad and disappointed that such a nice and suitable friendship for Pat had come to nothing. And Pat shared her feelings, for a while. Then he decided that he was definitely off women for the foreseeable future, and when Ossie invited him to join him in another trip to Fairhaven Pat said he would prefer to save his cash, rather than hand it over to some old bag who probably had the clap anyway.

A fairly lengthy period of austerity and hard work then ensued, and he was flogging himself so persistently that Emmie became worried about him. It wasn't natural and healthy for a young man like him to slog away so hard, it was surely bad for his health, it would make him old before his time, and much more in the same vein.

One midday he was working on a car in the large garage attached to the Reef Hotel. Artie, the young errand boy who liked to think of himself as the hotel porter, appeared with one of the Hotel trucks, loaded with bags and cases.

'We got a bit of class moving into one of them bungalows down on the bay,' said Artie. 'Mrs Enid Porter, that's the name on her bags, but she's travelling on her own. I reckon she's an actress or one of them sexy bits you see on the telly – she's got everything it takes to turn a guy on, if you see what I mean.'

Using both hands he sketched some highly voluptuous shapes in the air. 'Boy what I'd like to do to her!'

'You're frothing, sonny,' said Pat. 'If you don't watch out you'll rupture yourself.'

'Up yours,' said Artie and towed his load around to the road.

Pat went back to his work, patching up a defective exhaust system. That Artie was sure a randy little runt, always kidding himself he'd be a welcome treat to a grown woman. Pat recollected that he had probably been the same when he was fourteen or so.

THREE

It was not until a couple of days later that he saw Mrs Enid Porter, and then it happened by accident. The path that followed the coast line was part of the right of way to the Reef Hotel; at one place it crossed a little stream by way of a foot-bridge, an imitation rustic wooden job. Somebody had lately tugged away part of the railing, and Charlie Olestead had instructed Pat to repair the damage.

Pat spent a leisurely morning on the job, working without his shirt in the sun. He had nearly finished the railing when he saw her coming along the path, and he immediately appreciated what young Artie had been getting at. This was a woman you had to look at. She was obviously used to being looked at, and she liked it – you could tell that. Not the shy reserved type. Hell, no.

She wore cream slacks, and a tight blue jersey under which her breasts were nicely free. Graceful, that was the right word for her. She had thick blonde hair, kind of streaky, and clear blue eyes that were giving him a comprehensive appraisal as she approached the little bridge.

She smiled pleasantly, and said, 'you make a good advertisement for the sunshine here, all that healthy tan...'

He grinned and straightened up so that she could note his impressive development.

'Have a nice visit on the Reef, Mrs Porter,' he said. 'I heard your name up at the Hotel yesterday, I'm Pat Quiney.'

'You live here?'

'I do,' he said.

'I envy you,' she said. 'I expect I'll see you around, Pat.'

'You bet,' he said. He watched her walk on up the path. She was a lovely mover, and already he was back at the old game, imagining what she would look like without her clothes. During the next few days he found plenty of excuses for hanging around the little bay; he knew which bungalow she was using, and several times he caught sight of her, walking along the beach, or sitting out there on the rocks, writing or drawing something on a pad. Once he saw her walking across the sand for a swim; and her costume was so skimpy and tight that she might as well have been naked. And she was a terrific performer in the water. He had only spoken to her once, and he couldn't stop thinking about her.

He was a little disappointed to discover that she had friends on the Reef. Pat had never had any dealings with Tim Taggart and his sister Vera. They didn't mix much with ordinary folk on the Reef, but they called on Mrs Porter and had her up to their place on the cliffs. Pat had seen her in their beach buggy, it was the only one on the Reef. Tim Taggart had a pretty nifty cruiser, but Pat had never had the chance to go over it or do any work on it. The Taggarts had money, but most folk reckoned they were a strange pair. Brother and sister? Some folk didn't believe that. They came and they went, and nobody on the Reef knew much about them, least of all where their money came from, because Tim Taggart never seemed to do any work. They weren't all that popular on the Reef.

Matt Higgins, a friend of Pat's from school, owned a sailing dinghy, which he was able to use only at weekends since he worked during the week in a real estate office in Fairhaven. He let Pat use the dinghy in the week, in return for keeping it in good sailing shape. It was a friendly arrangement, and whenever he felt he could spare a couple of hours and the wind was right, Pat would take the dinghy out and around the Reef.

One afternoon he sailed along the coast and round to the little bay. There was a fresh breeze, and he came into the bay pretty fast. She lay face-down on the rocks, spread out on a towel, she was taking the sun, and her body was shining and nude.

He made all the clatter he could, letting the sail flap noisily in the wind. She sat up, pulled a white singlet over her head, and deftly got into some shorts, ignoring him until she was clothed.

Then she waved.

'Like a sail?' he called out.

She thought for a moment, then called back, 'I'd love it.' She collected her gear and made her way along the rocks to where he had the dinghy waiting. He gave her a hand as she stepped neatly aboard and settled beside him. There was very little room in the dinghy's stern, and he had to have his arm around her in order to handle the tiller.

The dinghy dipped under the breeze, and went scudding out across the bay. Her blonde hair blew against his face and she laughed.

'Sorry,' she said. 'I like your boat.'

'Not mine,' he said. 'Just borrowed. Have you done much sailing, Mrs Porter?'

'A little,' she said. 'My name is Enid, by the way – we don't need to be formal, do we, Pat? A bit silly in the circumstances, don't you agree?'

'Yes,' he said.

They had got clear of the bay and now they were heading along the coast.

'I'm sorry I interrupted your sun-bathing,' he said.

'I'm not,' she said. 'This is much more fun.'

'I'll teach you to steer,' he said, 'if you like...'

'Later,' she said. 'I'm enjoying this.'

'Me too,' said Pat, and set out to demonstrate the dinghy's best paces in the open sea. It was exhilarating, a light-hearted and no-holds-barred excursion, when the dinghy began to dance around, and there is no quicker way to get to know somebody than by sharing the chores and limited accommodation of a sailing dinghy in a fair breeze.

She was a lively companion, and at no time did Pat feel that the difference in their ages mattered at all. She was a married woman and she didn't talk about her husband, and that was okay with Pat. He gathered that she might be making a longish stay on the Reef, and that also was very much okay with him.

She was easily the most elegant and attractive woman he had come across, and she was treating him like an equal, a man who interested her. It was a flattering experience.

It was late in the afternoon when they got back to the bay, and he had to refuse her invitation to have a little refreshment with her in her bungalow because he wanted to get the dinghy back in the harbour before dark; the afternoon breeze had died away and it could take him some hours to get back.

'Next time,' he said, 'we'll arrange things better.'

She smiled. The dinghy had drifted close up to the rocks and she could step ashore with ease.

'Thank you for the voyage,' she said. Leaning forward quickly she kissed him, a light butterfly of a kiss, and then she was ashore.

'Tomorrow,' he said. 'Earlier–'

'Perhaps,' she said. 'But don't you have to work, Pat? You can't spend all your time taking me around...'

He grinned. 'I don't see why not.' He loosed the sail and the dinghy tilted and began to move out and across the bay. He watched her until the rise of the rocks hid her from view.

He was still remembering the excitement she had roused in him when he eased the dinghy up to its mooring in the harbour; it was dusk and he was late for supper, but Emmie didn't mind, he had been out in the fresh air sailing, and she approved of that. He was happy, she could tell that, and that was good. When he was moody around the house he was unbearable. He needed a holiday.

The next morning he brought the dinghy into the bay just on midday. He couldn't see her at first, she was not sun-bathing on the rocks. He ran the dinghy up on the beach and tugged it clear of the water. He went across the sand and it was all pretty scorching in the sun; he wore nothing but shorts, and a sweater knotted around his middle like a loose apron.

When he saw her she was sitting on her verandah, waiting for him. She wore a blue bathing suit and she had a sketching-pad on her knee. She held up her hand.

'Just stop there, please,' she said. 'Relax and try not to move, squint if you like, but don't move, and throw that silly sweater away...'

He halted in the hot loose sand and undid the sweater and tossed it to one side.

'Okay if I grin?'

She nodded, she was sketching quickly, frowning now and then.

'It's hot as the hinges of hell out here,' he said.

'Okay, okay,' she said, and some sweating minutes later she told him he could move.

He stood beside her and looked at the sketch she had done of him; it was rough, but he could recognise himself.

'Can I have it?' he said. 'I think it's good.'

'It's rubbish,' she said. 'I'll do a better one when I have more time. Let's go inside and have a nice cool drink.'

He followed her across the verandah and into her living-room, and she went into the kitchen to collect the beer. Pat glanced at some drawings that were on the table; there were sketches of the sea and the rocks, and trees, and one of a naked woman that caught his immediate attention. He was still looking at it with considerable interest when Enid came out with the cans of beer and glasses.

He looked at her, and there was no embarrassment in her face, just a faint hint of some amusement.

'This is you,' he said, and knew it was not a very clever observation.

'Naked and unashamed,' she said lightly. She took the drawing from him and put it with the others. She gave him a can of beer and a glass.

'I flattered myself,' she said.

'No,' he said. 'That's not a bad drawing, but you're beautiful.'

She poured some beer into her glass and drank it slowly.

'I'd like to draw you,' she said, 'but you'd be too shy, wouldn't you? In what they call the altogether?'

It was her smile that decided him. He drank his beer straight from the can, all of it in one unbroken swallow. He placed the can on the table very deliberately.

'What's there to be shy about?' he said. 'In here or outside?'

'The chair by the window,' she said.

It was a lounging-chair with an extended

foot-rest and some cushions. There was another just like it out on the verandah.

'Make yourself comfortable,' she said. 'We won't be disturbed.' She gave him a quick reassuring smile, and went into her bedroom.

He took off his shorts and arranged himself on the chair, with the cushions piled at his head. He thought he would feel nervous while he waited, and he had draped his shorts across his middle.

When she came out she had put on a short skirt, and she had more drawing materials. She laughed. 'Oh Pat,' she said, 'are you going to be coy after all?'

He threw the shorts over the chair. She nodded, and fussed with the curtains so that the sunlight was funnelled over the chair. She made him sit up while she fixed the cushions the way she wanted them.

'Now I just want you to relax, all of you,' she said. 'Imagine you are absolutely on your own in the room, thinking nice thoughts, you get the idea?'

She had seated herself by the table with her drawing-pad and already she was looking at him fixedly, only to break off now and then to make some sweeping lines on the paper.

'You're still too tense,' she said. 'Forget everything here, go to sleep – I've seen a naked man before, I've been in a life class in the States, you're okay, Pat.'

'Thanks, how long will this take?'

'As long as it has to,' she said. 'If you want to go to the bathroom just yell.'

'I thought we'd go for a sail,' he said.

'Plenty of time for that,' she said. 'Flex your left leg just a little, but keep the pose lazy.'

There were several rejected sheets before she appeared satisfied with the way the work was going. Mostly she ignored him completely for long busy periods. He would never have believed he could lie naked like this in front of an attractive woman without giving himself away. It would be sure to happen. He had his eyes closed and he was concentrating on other things, pretending he was not there. It was a bit like being in a doctor's surgery, except that he had never so far come across a doctor who looked like Enid.

He could hear the tide on the shore, and now and then her chair creaked. This wasn't the kind of episode he could boast about to Ossie, or anybody else on the Reef for that matter. Ossie would fall about laughing at the idea.

'Okay, that's it,' she said. 'It's pretty lousy, but it's the best I can do. You can come to life again, Pat.'

'I'm not sorry that's over,' he said reaching for his shorts. 'I thought I might disgrace myself.'

She laughed, and gave him the drawing. He looked at it, and then at her. 'I'd like to keep it,' he said.

'I'd rather have it back,' she said. 'Perhaps I'll do some more of you another time. This one isn't for passing around among your friends.'

'I wouldn't think of it,' he said. 'It's me all right—'

'With no fig leaf.' She smiled as she took the drawing back. 'Tempting, but forbidden – I'm too old for you, Pat. Much too old.'

'I've never known anybody like you,' he said, and reached out for her.

She slipped past him. 'We're going sailing,' she said, 'remember? So let's not have the wrestling match, okay? I don't usually eat at midday, but I'll make us a little picnic.'

She collected up all her drawings and put them into a folder and took them back into her bedroom. Then she loaded a basket with cans of beer, biscuits and fruit. He carried the basket out into the sunshine and they went down the sand to the dinghy.

'I expect you've made plenty of drawings of men like that,' he said before he ran the dinghy out.

'Hundreds,' she said, and laughed again. 'Pat, just how old are you?'

'Old enough.'

'Now I've hurt your feelings, I'm sorry, I didn't mean to,' she said. 'Doing that sketch was a mistake. Let's forget it.'

This time she wasn't interested in any navigation tuition; she squatted between his knees, her arms on his thighs, and her legs stretched out. It was not a posture that Pat could object to. He could feel her breathing, and the movement of her chest when she spoke and laughed. When he stroked her cheek and shoulder and the curve of her arm she didn't object either. There was little conversation.

She unpacked the basket and handed food and drink up to him. It was all very jolly and festive. They were clear of the bay and the dinghy was making a fair speed. She turned to look up at him, and he bent and kissed her, a long and very searching kiss that met with complete co-operation from her, while the dinghy lost way and the nylon sail flapped and cracked.

'Pat,' she said eventually, 'we're not being very bright about this.'

'It had to happen,' he said. 'We both know that.'

Now he had gripped her tightly between his knees and the dinghy came upright and steady for a moment before falling away again to slop about untidily in the water, and Pat hoped there was nobody watching who knew how the dinghy should be handled. He reached down for her breasts, and she covered his hands with her own.

'Now Pat,' she said, 'this is developing into an indecent assault.'

He said nothing, and when she took her hands away he slid the straps of her blue swimsuit off her shoulders, and now he really did feel her. She whispered something that he did not hear, but he knew she was beginning to respond.

'This isn't quite the right situation, is it?' she said softly. 'You're being masterful all of a sudden – let's go back, please...'

He let her put her straps back, he brought the dinghy smartly about, and they were heading for the bay again. He caught all the breeze there was, and the dinghy seemed to share some of their urgency, so that they were returning much faster than they had set out.

Pat beached the dinghy with unseaman-like speed, and they both tugged it clear, then went up the sand, holding hands, hurrying.

They were a pair of eager lovers, heading for bliss. She towed him across the verandah and into her living-room, and her face was alight with anticipation as she turned to him. He folded his arms about her, and this time there was going to be no mistake, and she was going to know what she was about to get, the big *macho* treatment. He practically had her off her feet already, and then over her shoulder he happened to glance out of the window.

'Hell,' he said, 'look who's coming. We got company, that's fat old Taggart.'

'So it is,' she said, and she did not appear too annoyed or surprised. 'He's early – what a bore the man is...'

'You mean you knew he was coming?' demanded Pat. 'You never said – I thought we were going to have the afternoon together.'

They were no longer tangled in a tight and loving embrace, and Pat was scowling.

'What am I supposed to do?' he said angrily.

'Just be sensible, please,' she said. 'You can't be jealous of Tim, I've known him and his sister for years. He's come to collect me, that's all.'

'I still think it's a lousy deal for me,' said Pat.

She put her hand over his mouth, and she spoke quickly as she said, 'Tomorrow evening, walk, you won't be needing the boat – okay? Now behave nice and normal when he arrives – promise?'

'Something will happen to foul things up tomorrow night,' he said.

She laughed and gave him a quick kiss. 'Be nice,' she whispered.

Tim Taggart was coming along the coast path, and now he had emerged from the trees. He wore a Palm Beach suit, and carried the jacket folded tidily over his arm; he wore a Panama hat tilted jauntily, and he smoked a cigar. With his heavy moustache and his prominent belly, he was an impressive figure. A wealthy gentleman strolling at his leisure by the seashore.

'He looks like some goddam Hollywood gangster,' said Pat, and Enid had to suppress a giggle as she went out to meet Tim.

'I didn't expect you so soon,' she said.

'I left the buggy back there on the road,' said Tim, and decided not to give Enid the usual perfunctory kiss by way of a greeting because of the openly hostile look the young feller was giving him. He nodded at Pat and said, 'I know you, don't I?'

'This is Pat Quiney,' said Enid.

'You work around the Reef Hotel and the harbour, sometimes, correct?'

'Correct,' said Pat.

'Nice to meet you,' said Tim. He took off his Panama and said to Enid, 'I could use a cool drink, baby.' And he walked into her living-room.

'See you soon, Pat,' said Enid.

'Maybe,' he said, and left without bothering about any farewell.

Tim joined her on the verandah; he had got himself a beer, and his free hand automatically slipped around her waist. Pat was plunging down the beach to the dinghy.

'You're scraping the barrel a bit, baby,'

said Tim. 'He's just a kid. Have you had him in the sack yet?'

She twitched herself free. 'Would you like to hear what he called you just now? "Fat old Taggart" – very suitable, I thought.'

Tim's cigar had gone out, and he tossed it down onto the dry sand. 'Now I'll tell you something,' he said pleasantly. 'You're getting to be an old bag. Just a few more years, and then you'll be on the junk heap. Never let yourself forget that, honey lamb. Once your looks are gone you're nothing but a liability.'

She shrugged. She had heard it all before. He followed her through to the door of her bedroom. She stopped him there, looked at him with no emotion whatsoever and said simply, 'No.'

He knew she was not in the mood to be coaxed. So maybe she and the kid had just had a roll in the hay, which he had interrupted by arriving unexpectedly early. The notion amused Tim, and he gave her a wide lascivious grin. 'Pardon me, lady, how was the kid?'

She slammed the door in his face. She would be more amenable later, she always was; she might put on an act, but the fact was that she couldn't do without it, plenty of it. And she could still look like a million dollars when there was some sex in view, and the Quiney kid might be a youngster, but he had the build, and he would have the enthusiasm to go with it.

She kept him waiting. She spent a long time in the bathroom under the shower before she even started to get dressed, and Tim knew that was never a quick operation; Enid took care of her appearance. He wandered out onto the verandah and watched young Quiney out there with his boat in the bay; he was handling it pretty smartly, and he was supposed to be a bit of a wizard on most types of engines. A local boy, picking up a dollar here and there – and maybe expecting to screw a doll like Enid? The kid should be so lucky.

FOUR

Pat was not a happy young man as he sailed the dinghy around the coast. He was angry and frustrated, and in the mood to break something, preferably that old bastard Taggart's jaw. If he had arrived just a few minutes later at the bungalow he would certainly have found them in bed. No doubt about that. Pat snorted with amusement at the mental picture of himself all tangled up with Enid in her bed, and Taggart would be gawping at them in the doorway. It was a pity it hadn't turned out like that.

Enid had him worried, because she should have been more annoyed and put out when Taggart had come on the scene so early, and he wondered again just how well she knew Taggart. He seemed to be very much at home in her bungalow. So all in all, Pat was working up a steaming head of hate about Tim Taggart. He was an easy guy to hate, and he acted so goddamn pleased with himself. Pat shied away from the notion that Enid could ever have been more than just a friend to Taggart. It wasn't possible.

That evening after supper he went out for a stroll. The Reef Hotel was too pricey for him as a rule, but this time he looked in at one of the two bars, and bought a lager which he seldom drank, the Hotel bar sold little beer. He knew his way around the place because of the many jobs he had done there. In the dining-room he saw the three of them, Enid and the two Taggarts, and he made sure they didn't see him. Enid looked terrific, bare shoulders and her hair shining in the soft light. She appeared to be having a very good time. Vera Taggart looked like a female wrestler in a figured dress. And Tim Taggart in that Palm Beach outfit was clearly bossing the show.

Another interesting item was that Charlie Olestead was hovering around their table, and before Pat moved off Olestead had taken the fourth chair, and Tim Taggart didn't seem to mind. So a party might be in the offing, in one of the Hotel rooms. They happened, and they were rumoured to be pretty ripe affairs. Pat had never been to one. You needed money, and a working stiff like Pat Quiney could never expect to get an invitation, nor did he ever want one, so he told himself.

He walked down the hill to the harbour, he saw the Sinclair car parked outside the *Jolly Sailor,* so he went on walking, he was not in the mood for Ossie Sinclair, and he remembered the last time he had been drinking in the *Jolly Sailor* with Ossie – a disaster that still made him squirm. He didn't trust himself where Ossie was concerned – they'd have some drinks and Ossie would push the pace up and before he knew it Pat would be talking about Enid, and Ossie would surely find that very funny. And then Pat would probably have to punch him in the mouth to even things up.

So Pat dropped into a pub near the quay, called, believe it or not, the *Lobster Pot.* One of the harbour tarts made him an offer, but without much conviction because she knew who he was, he bought her a small rum. After a couple of beers he bought a pair of bottles of beer and a paper bag to carry them in.

He went down the coast path, and when

he came to Enid's bungalow he found himself a comfortable spot by the bushes; he could watch the path, and when he saw her coming he would decide how to handle the situation. The Taggarts might walk down with her, leaving their buggy up on the road. Or just Tim Taggart might be with her ... a possibility that Pat did not like thinking about.

She would be glad to see him after that fiasco in the afternoon. If she wasn't alone he wouldn't embarrass her. He would wait until she was alone.

He tried to make the beer last, but the two bottles didn't go all that far. He lay back and gazed up at the starlit sky. He dozed a little. He took a succession of cautious short walks along the sand, ready to hop into cover as soon as he heard her coming. There were the usual noises from the sea and the trees, the quirking of birds sleeping ... lots of blue-black night all around.

He walked around the bungalow and tried the doors at the back and the front, and they were locked, as he had expected. He retreated to his burrow by the trees, and eventually he went to sleep although all along he had been telling himself that he was not there to sleep and he could discipline himself into keeping awake as long as he had to, it was a question of will-power. It didn't work. He awoke chilled and stiff, and in sour mood. It was nearly three in the morning.

He cursed himself and made another check on the bungalow in case she had returned while he was asleep. It was all locked up as before. He could see into her bedroom because the curtains hadn't been drawn, and there was nobody in the bed. She was sleeping elsewhere, at the Reef Hotel, or maybe with the Taggarts. The hell with it. He was making a fool of himself. She had him dangling on a string, and he didn't matter in the least.

He started back up the coast path, and his mind was no longer engaged on erotic imaginings in which Mrs Enid Porter was scheduled to be a willing partner.

All the Reef was asleep, except him. He met nobody, until he reached the small square where there were a few shops, and a tiny parking-place; it was empty of vehicles.

He had crossed into a side road where there were no street lights, when a sudden shaft of light caught him full in the face and then travelled over his body before it was turned off.

'Hell,' said Pat, 'You don't have to do that.'

'Now take it easy, sport.' The man with the torch was one of the Reef's three patrolmen; there was also a Sergeant resident on the Reef, and a Lieutenant who lived in Fairhaven and visited the Reef when required, which was not very often. The patrolmen were local boys, and Pat knew this one. Abie Garrett.

'You're out late, Pat,' said Abie. 'What's the score?'

Pat held up his hands in mock surrender. Abie was keen after promotion, they said; he was a couple of years older than Pat.

'You been out drinking somewhere, Pat?'

'Even you can see I'm sober,' said Pat, 'and I haven't been breaking into enclosed premises either, I'm just out enjoying the night air, if that's okay with you.'

Abie Garrett moved in a shade closer. He was a thin streak of a man, ambitious and full of suspicion about other folks, especially young men who walked abroad at night and gave police officers sassy answers.

'You been chasing it up with some woman, that right? Does Aunt Emmie know you're out this late?'

'Why don't you take a jump into the harbour?' said Pat.

'I could take you in for questioning,' said Abie. 'Law-abiding citizens don't wander around at this time of the night without a reasonable explanation. So what's yours, Pat Quiney?'

'Just walking for exercise,' said Pat. 'I'd like to see you prove otherwise, Abie my boy. I expect I'd resist arrest and work you over a bit, and then the Lieutenant would come over from Fairhaven and throw the book at you for wrongful arrest. Mind how you go.'

Pat walked off, and Abie let him go. But Abie was sure that the time would come when he would have the drop on Pat Quiney, it was bound to happen, and then he would let him have it. Teach him some respect for Law and Order.

Pat hoped to get to his bed with no more bother. Aunt Emmie met him as he was climbing the stairs; she was a tiny woman, but in her long nightdress and dressing-gown, standing at the head of the stairs, she made a formidable figure.

'Pat,' she said frostily, 'it's nearly four o'clock, where have you been? I've been sick with worry–'

'Just out walking,' he said, 'down along by the shore. Nothing to worry about, honestly, Auntie – I haven't been in any trouble, you can see that – I just felt like a stroll by my-self...'

He had climbed the stairs and he stood beside her. She was relieved to note that there was no smell of drink on him, not really, and she could tell he hadn't been spending the night with some woman, she was sure of that also.

'I don't like this kind of behaviour from you, Pat,' she said. 'You worry me, and you shouldn't–'

'Sorry,' he said, and he really meant it.

'If you were in trouble, you'd tell me,

wouldn't you?' she said. 'If you've got something on your mind–'

'You're a dear old thing,' he said, and slipped one arm around her to walk her back to her bedroom. 'I just didn't think you might be worried when I stayed out ambling around the beach – I promise I won't do it again.'

He stopped and kissed her.

'Be good,' she said, and went off to bed.

Although he was tired Pat had some trouble getting to sleep. He had done better down on the beach when he should have been keeping watch on her bungalow. He thought about Abie Garrett and regretted not saying the crushing things he could now remember. Over breakfast the next morning Aunt Emmie said nothing about the escapade of the previous night; she had the virtue, rare in most women, of knowing when not to drag an unpleasant topic up again.

Pat had a number of jobs that kept him busy all through the day. As he now saw it, his recent brief vacation was over; he had work to do, profitable work. So he did not intend to waste any more of his time dancing attendance on Mrs Enid Porter, only to get himself elbowed out in favour of some old bastard like Taggart.

If Enid was prepared to play hard to get she could keep it all to herself, and that would be okay with Pat Quiney. You bet.

The day passed very satisfactorily. He replaced a wooded window-frame and rehung a door, and got paid cash then and there. Very nice. There was an engine job on a cruiser for tomorrow, and for a new client, Pat always liked working for a new client – they usually settled on the spot, and he would do extra special work.

He found it one hell of a long evening, and he felt edgy and restless. After supper Emmie said she would have an early night; she liked her sleep, and last night had been interrupted, although once again she didn't lodge any boring complaint. Pat said he might take a walk, but he wouldn't be late. And he meant it.

It was dark when he strolled down the hill to the waterfront. He avoided the pubs where he might meet anybody he knew, like Ossie for instance. He sat on the quay for a while, looking at the ships in the harbour, and the lights dancing on the water, very pretty. There were party sounds coming from one of the larger cabin cruisers; *Penelope* wasn't a locally owned craft, she was all gleaming white paint and metal fittings, and her owner came from down the coast, one of the few genuine playboys to visit the Reef. He travelled with his own women. What a way to live.

Later Pat watched some of the fishing boats setting out from the harbour; they were more in his line, in fact at one time he had thought of trying to own a boat and fish for a living. But Emmie hadn't been encouraging; there wasn't much money in fishing nowadays, not for a fisherman working with one small boat.

Shortly after ten o'clock he found himself on the coast path; he told himself it was an accident and he knew he wasn't fooling himself. He didn't turn back, and it wasn't going to mean anything.

She would have forgotten that she had invited him to visit her, and not to be too early. So he would walk around her place, and then head for home. There were lights on in her bungalow, and as he drew nearer his heart was beginning to hammer against his ribs. And he made a fairly noisy approach across her verandah.

The door opened before he reached it, and there she was welcoming him with arms outstretched and the most inviting of smiles. She wore a clinging pyjama suit, peachy pale, with no sleeves and cut low in front, and her breasts made twin tents in the thin material.

She drew him in and kicked the door shut and wound her arms around his neck.

'I thought you weren't going to come,' she said. 'I was having some horrible thoughts about you, darling Pat.'

'I don't think anything would have kept me

away,' he said, thrusting all his earlier hesitation clean out of his mind. She wanted him just as much as he wanted her, and already he knew that she wore nothing under those pyjamas that slid away under his hand and revealed the lovely warm woman and her smooth skin.

She made him sit it the lounging-chair in which she had sketched him.

'Now what are we going to drink?' she said. 'Beer, whisky – I've even got a spot of brandy, what's it to be?'

'Would you mind if I said coffee?'

She laughed, stopped and gave him a quick kiss. 'Of course not,' she said. 'We'll both have coffee.'

She went into the kitchen, and after a while he followed her. She stood by the stove, and he held her, with her back against him and his hands over her breasts. He kissed her neck, and she turned into his embrace. She reached out and put the stove off so that the coffee would come to no grief because of what they were intending to do.

'We're wasting time,' she whispered, and they went into her bedroom. 'Hurry, darling – hurry now!'

With a gesture of wild abandon she whipped off her pyjama top and tossed it across the room, and then she slid herself sinuously out of the trousers, and she posed provocatively for a moment, smiling at him.

'Will I do?' she asked. 'Are you disappointed, Pat Quiney?'

'I've never seen anything so beautiful,' he said, and his mouth had suddenly become dry.

She smiled at the note of awe in his voice. He really was young and so inexperienced. She sat on the edge of the bed. This was going to be pleasant and quite rewarding. He had a nice body, fresh and healthy. Eager, and that was flattering when she remembered that she was probably twice his age. Some goddess of beauty.

She patted the bed; he had undressed and he came over and sat beside her. He was shy, but it was passing.

'You strip well,' she said, 'if I may mention the matter. But already I know that, don't I?'

He gently eased her down onto the bed, then placed himself beside her.

'You're beautiful,' he said.

She pulled his head down so that she could kiss him, and then moved over so that he covered her. He made love to her, and it was over too quickly to be anything memorable. She went out into the kitchen and came back in a couple of minutes with two mugs of coffee on a tray.

'I'm sorry,' he said. 'I wasn't much good, was I?'

'Don't say that, it was nice,' she said, 'and

it will be better next time.'

She heaped the pillows at the head of the double bed, and they sat together and drank the coffee. It was very pleasant.

'You weren't here last night,' he said. 'I came down and I waited outside for a long time, but you didn't come back... I hoped I'd see you. Where did you sleep?'

She glanced at him briefly. 'I don't have to answer that,' she said, 'but I will. I had dinner at the Reef Hotel with the Taggarts, and I went back to their place afterwards. I've told you, Pat, they're old friends, both of them, and it's too silly if you're going to be jealous of Tim.'

'I'm jealous of any man who's a friend of yours. Okay, so it's silly, but it's the way I am about you.'

'I ought to send you home,' she said slowly. 'I don't think I'm going to be good for you.'

'I wouldn't go,' he said. 'You're lumbered with me now. I intend to hang around.'

He moved down the bed. With the tips of his fingers he began to explore the smooth skin of her thigh next to him.

'You're wonderful,' he murmured, and his voice was almost reverent.

She ruffled his hair and told him he was a pet. He desperately hoped she wasn't going to ask him how many women he had been to bed with and how much experience he'd had of the naked female body and its delights. But she wasn't Mollie, she didn't ask any questions that he mightn't want to answer, and she had the kind of body that made Mollie nothing but a scrawny and unattractive scrubber. Enid had class. She was marvellous to look at. A knock-out. She smelt good and she felt good.

She slid down the bed to join him. She had been so right – it was better the next time, it was the stuff they made poems about. Oh boy this was really it.

They slept a little afterwards. She said it wouldn't be advisable if he stayed all night. There were going to be plenty of other nights, and he liked hearing her say that. Because he couldn't imagine what it would be like if he couldn't go on making love to her night after night. He wanted to kiss all of her over and over. He finally tore himself away and went happily out into the night. Taller and more masterful than ever before. It wasn't all that late, just coming up to one o'clock.

He was in very good spirits. He had achieved something – he had made love, twice, that night to a gorgeous and sophisticated woman. The course of his life had altered, and even to think of her excited and aroused him.

Meeting Abie Garrett who was still on the graveyard shift did nothing to take the shine off the occasion for Pat.

'Hiya, old sport,' said Abie, and this time he didn't have to do the constabulary business with his torch because they had met under one of the few street lamps. 'Sleep-walking again, Pat? You'd better do something about that. You could get yourself into trouble, wandering about the town in the small hours.'

Pat just grinned at him.

'It's a woman,' said Abie. 'Two nights in a row – she must be pretty hot.'

'You've got a dirty mind that goes with that uniform,' said Pat. 'If ever I meet you and you're not on duty, Abie, I'll be happy to push your face in, okay?'

'I have my eye on you,' said Abie severely. 'You put a foot wrong, and I'll have you for sure, Pat Quiney.'

'In a pig's eye,' said Pat, and walked off. This time he got up to his room without arousing Aunt Emmie, and he slept the sound sleep of a young lecher, debauched and totally contented.

Over the next ten days or so this became the pattern of his life. She wouldn't let him come to her every night, no matter how much he urged her, and if he visited her on the off-chance that she might be in he might find the bungalow empty. She pointed out that she had some social life of her own on the Reef, and she wasn't going to let his attentions swamp her – she made that clear to him quite nicely.

They went to bed together fairly frequently, sometimes in the afternoon – but he was never to take her for granted. He was becoming a satisfactory lover, she told him that as well, and allowed him to demonstrate – to their mutual enjoyment.

Aunt Emmie noticed the change in him – his fits of moodiness at home, and his reluctance to tell her sometimes where he had been; he wasn't doing much work, even though he was out of the house for long periods. He didn't stay out late, not really, and he wasn't drinking. She guessed he had a girl down in the town somewhere. In his own good time she hoped he would talk to her, and bring the girl home.

There was no confusion now in Pat Quiney's mind. He was in love, it was a red-hot scorching passion, and he would never be the same man again – it had marked him for the rest of his life.

Enid Porter was the one and only, she filled all his waking thoughts. Not just sex, but love, the real thing. He planned all sorts of things for their future. Away from the Reef, soon, and she would find she couldn't do without him. So what the hell did the difference in their ages matter? He wouldn't let her ever get tired of him. Nobody would ever come between them.

He was in a pub early one evening, with Ossie Sinclair and a few of the guys, when Abie Garrett came in; he wasn't in uniform. He bought himself a beer and came over uninvited to join the party.

'How's your love life, Pat?' he said, and to the others, 'You know we have here the stallion of Roker's Reef, he's been putting it to some lucky little lady night after night for the last couple of weeks.'

'Is that so, Pat?' said Ossie. 'I thought you were off women?'

Abie Garret laughed. Pat stood up and shunted Abie hard against the wall, with one hand planted on Abie's chest.

'I warned you the other night,' he said. 'You button your trap or I'll smear you down this goddam wall – you get me?'

Before the rest of the party could intervene, and none of them hurried because Pat was really steaming and nobody would grieve over Abie, Pat had freed him, and Abie had retreated out of the pub, thinking hostile thoughts, but saying no more.

'You've got it bad, sport, who is she?' said Ossie.

Pat shrugged and walked out. He and Enid had been discreet, they had never been in the town together, or in any of the pubs. They had done some sailing around the coast, but that was safe enough. They had met nobody they knew on the beach or out on the water, and most of Pat's visits to the bungalow took place after dark. But the Reef wasn't all that big, and they both knew they couldn't hope to keep their affair a secret for much longer.

In fact, a whisper probably reached Aunt Emmie from somebody in her extensive circle of friends and customers – gabby females who missed little of what might be happening with a sniff of sex to it. She announced that she would be closing the store for a week, while they took their annual vacation and visited Lucy Baker in Oregon City. Lucy was Emmie's oldest friend, and she was approaching retirement as matron to a large hospital.

Pat did his best to wriggle out of the trip, but Emmie could be an obdurate little lady when she chose. Pat was going to accompany her, otherwise Lucy's feelings would be hurt, and that was that.

Pat was bored throughout the visit, although there were amenities that should have helped him to pass the time pleasantly. There were tennis courts in the hospital grounds, but Pat was an inept and unenthusiastic performer; there were few courts on the Reef, and he hadn't held a racket since leaving high school. What made it all the more mortifying was that his partner or his opponent might be one of the attractive young nurses from the hospital, and all of them could wipe the court with him, no matter what his biceps and chest measurements might be.

He could have found some fun, but he was not in the mood. He couldn't concentrate on anything or anybody, Enid filled his mind, and he thought about the marvellous times they'd had together, and would have again, as soon as he had her in his arms.

The bungalow on the Reef had no phones, so he couldn't talk to her and she had told him not to write to her because a letter might go astray, and no mail was delivered, it had to be collected from the Reef post office, so it would be better if he didn't write to her.

It was a long week, a hell of a long week, a penance. The only compensation was that Lucy Barker provided good food, and she never asked any fool questions when she could see that he didn't want to talk. She was okay. In private Aunt Emmie harangued him about being more polite and amenable, and so on. It surely was one drag of a week.

When he got back he found that things had changed. An interloper had appeared.

FIVE

Bastable Walker and Associates had their head office in Moorgate, in the City of London, and their interests were spread around the world. They could finance and control construction and building projects on a large scale – bridges, harbours, tunnels, urban developments, roads.

Their reputation was high, and their resources made it possible for them to deal with Governments abroad as often as with private firms. They had prestige, and their representatives on their travels found most important doors open to them, including those of H.M. Embassies in foreign parts.

Among their bright young men one of the brightest was reckoned to be David Archibald Firth. At thirty-six he kept himself in good condition, and he was considered by his immediate bosses to be a talented and highly intelligent young man who would surely rise to the top one day. Already he was carrying the kind of responsibilities that were usually reserved for more senior executives.

An important point in his favour was that he was able to get on well with other people, and his associates found him ready to work round the clock when necessary. He had resilience and stamina, and he was competitive without being too full of himself.

He was about six feet tall, and carried himself easily since he was always in good shape and had no surplus weight.

He had just completed a lengthy and fairly involved liaison assignment in Canada and the States; he had covered a mileage that would have beaten many of his colleagues. Everything had slotted in very nicely, he was satisfied, and flattering comments had reached him from London.

He had been working flat-out for nearly a year, and a long summer leave was due to him. He was told to go on leave forthwith. Bastable Walker, and Associates, would manage without him for a month. That was an order from the Personnel Director.

David had been operating from the Vancouver office. The world was wide open to him – the Seychelles, the Bahamas, Rio, the Riviera, or wherever...

He decided he was going to find an out-of-the-way spot, where he just might make a start on the project that he had been privately nursing for some time.

He discussed the problem with Laura Rosen, an enterprising and knowledgeable brunette who had been working as his secretary. He had taken her to dinner on several occasions; she was decorative and entertaining and they had become good friends. He suspected that they could easily have become more than friends if he had made the right moves. And Laura would not have given him a knee where it would hurt most. It was less complicated to leave things as they were.

'I don't want another hotel room,' he said. 'I've had enough of hotels, I want somewhere quiet and peaceful, where I won't have to bother with other people.'

'You could try the morgue,' she said. 'Why the anti-social attitude? That doesn't sound like you, David.'

'For years I've been thinking I could write a book if I ever had the time to get down to it,' he said. 'This might be the opportunity to find out if I've been kidding myself. I've got a month, that should be long enough to make a start.'

She gave him a thoughtful look. 'You're serious? What kind of a book, David?'

'If it ever gets into print I'll send you a copy,' he said.

'Roker's Reef might be the place for you,' she said. 'The Reef Hotel has some beach bungalows, if you get one of them you can let the rest of the world roll by, pretty largely. In the social sense the place is dead.'

'So how come you know about it?' said David.

'I was there last year, for a week,' she said

dreamily. 'I should have married him. It was bliss, David.'

'If I go there it will be to work,' he said.

'You'll be safe enough,' she said. 'Would you like me to make a reservation for you? I'd love to come with you, but it would never do.'

Regretfully, he agreed with her. He promised to send her a post-card, and two days later he had moved into one of the beach bungalows that belonged to the Reef Hotel.

There were three of them, situated around a small bay, and an easy ten-minute stroll along a coast path to link up with the road to Reef Town and the Reef Hotel. The bungalows were intended for visitors who preferred their own company for a while, such as honeymoon couples, or those engaged on an irregular affair, such as Laura and the lover she should have married.

Domestic help was available, the furnishings were adequate, and tenants could buy provisions in the town, or take their meals at the Hotel.

On his arrival at the Hotel, after travelling over in the ferry, David had been accorded a very cordial reception from Charlie Olestead, the general manager of the place, who had insisted on showing him his bungalow while his luggage was being bought down in a trolley. Olestead had been very ingratiating, and it was evident that Laura had quoted the name of Bastable Walker to some effect.

David arranged to have his main evening meal at the Hotel, and Olestead readily undertook to see that a supply of suitable provisions would be sent down from the Hotel to stock up the bungalow's small refrigerator; also the travelling domestic help, Agnes, would be calling on him. Nothing would be too much trouble to ensure that David Firth's stay on Roker's Reef was pleasant and enjoyable in all respects.

In the course of the next few hours Olestead did his best to discover just why his visitor had come to the Reef, and David told him simply that he was there on a vacation. He had dinner that night at the Hotel, and had to put up with the uninvited company again of Olestead, and by that time David felt he had made a working assessment of the man – Olestead was worried, very worried, and insecure about himself, he was also not the kind of man you would trust with the petty cash, or a young typist doing overtime. He had the look of a lecher, and he had lost no time in telling David some jokes that had been dirty without being amusing.

It was brilliant sunshine the following morning when he strolled out onto his verandah. And sat on the rail, the beach and the bay were beautiful, and so was the figure of a woman wading out through the shallows; she had long tanned legs and swinging fair hair, and she wore a pale blue one-piece swimsuit, very tight and not quite decent.

She saw him, she smiled and waved, and she called out, 'Good-morning.' Then she turned out to the bay, fastening her white cap. They had the whole place to themselves.

He watched her swim away from the beach, and she was very good; she had a smooth and economical stroke that suggested she could keep it up for a long time. At one tip of the bay there was an outcrop of rocks and a little cliff, and she was heading there.

She reached the rocks, pulled herself up, took off her cap, and sat and faced the bright sea. David went back into his living-room. His typewriter reproached him, still packed in its case; there were notebooks and stacks of paper – everything there and awaiting his attention.

He knew what he was going to do. In his bedroom he changed into his swimming-trunks, and inspected himself in the mirror – there was no flab yet, he looked fairly tidy, he thought. Nothing to be ashamed of.

He padded across the warm sand and into the water; she saw him and waved. Why not? There was nobody else there.

He waded until the water was waist-deep, then he set off to show her some of his best racing crawl. She would be watching him, he thought, and she had already demonstrated that she was no novice in the water.

He had to ease off a bit before he had covered the full course, but he still finished in reasonable style. He anchored himself to a piece of rock and grinned up at her, and the foreshortened view he had of her in that skimpy swimsuit was more than interesting.

'Hullo,' he said, 'am I intruding?'

'Not a bit, welcome aboard, neighbour,' she said.

'Thanks.' He pulled himself up and out of the water. She was sitting on a small piece of flat rock, and he had to crowd her to make room for himself. She didn't seem to mind.

'This is nice,' he said, and he was pleasantly aware of the length of her thigh against him, and her hip. Her hair was fair and thick and shining in the sun. Blue eyes were smiling at him, and a wide generous mouth.

'You were running out of gas, back there,' she said. 'You need practice.'

'I do,' he said. 'You swim very well.'

'I ought to,' she said. 'I've been doing this little trip every day for some weeks now, and sometimes twice a day. It keeps me in shape.'

'Indeed it does,' he said.

'You're David Firth,' she said. 'Charlie Olestead at the Hotel told me you were coming.

We're the only two in the bungalows. I'm Enid Porter. Are you here on a vacation, Mr Firth?'

'Yes,' he said. 'Sort of.'

'You'll find it quiet,' he said. 'There's not a lot happens around here on the social scene.'

'That will suit me for a while,' he said.

'You're English.'

'I won't pretend otherwise,' he said. 'And you are a Canadian or an American?'

'American, from Seattle, believe it or not,' she said, and her smile widened and became even more friendly. 'My divorce came through a couple of months ago and the alimony has finally started to trickle my way – I'll have you know that my ex was one mean son of a bitch, so here I am on my lonesome, doing what I please and when I please. I'm kind of in training, setting myself up for my next phase, as another liberated lady. Maybe it'll be Acapulco, or Vegas – it'll sure be another kind of life for me, and when it comes I'll be good and ready for it. Does that sound crazy?'

'No,' he said. 'You know what you want, and I hope you'll get it.'

'But you don't think I will,' she said. 'That's the way you sounded. Tell me, are you married, Mr Firth?'

'Not any more.'

'You wouldn't care to elaborate on that?'

she said. 'Or is it none of my goddam business?'

'She left me,' he said. 'Seven years ago. I have no idea where she is or what she is doing, and I don't much care now. She had her own income, more than I was earning then. She evidently found me unsatisfactory in many ways, and she was never tired of telling me of my stupidities. We had lots of silly little quarrels that began to develop into serious rows, when we both tossed insults about. I was establishing myself in my job, it's pretty demanding, and I had to be away a lot. Whenever I came home we seemed to do nothing but wrangle. We had a flat in London, there were no children, which was probably just as well – they wouldn't have had much of a deal with the two of us. So there was another marriage that went phut. Mostly my fault, I expect.'

'Didn't you try to get her back?'

He shrugged. 'Not very hard. This must be boring for you to listen to.'

'I'm listening,' she said. 'I had a dud marriage myself.'

'I went through the motions of an abandoned husband,' he said, 'and I traced her to Italy. She was living in a villa near Florence, with an aunt of hers who had always considered me too ill-bred for her niece. The meeting was frigid all through. If I wanted to divorce her for desertion I had the name of her lawyers. She would never come back to me.'

'She had another guy, right?' said Enid.

'I don't know,' said David. 'She's not unpleasant to look at, and she has that comforting private income. If she does decide she wants to regularise the position, and perhaps get married again, I might decide to be as obstructive and awkward as I can, just for the hell of it. She thinks I'm a boor, selfish and inconsiderate – okay, that's the way I'll behave if I have to. She left me, it wasn't the other way around.'

'You have a point,' said Enid.

'She can still make me angry when I think of her,' he said. 'So I try not to think of her very often.'

'But you haven't sworn off women for good,' she said, and she gave him a shrewd inspection. 'You couldn't kid me on that.'

'You're so right,' he said.

'You're healthy,' she said, 'and you are not one of those closet queens or anything like that.'

'Absolutely not,' he said. 'I think lots of women are wonderful, but I don't have any plans to get married again. How about you? You've had a failure, and so have I, would you marry again?'

'I wouldn't bet against it,' she said. 'To tell you the truth, I've never lived alone for long. I get on okay with most men.'

The growing warmth of her thigh against him was beginning to disturb him in an unmistakable and pleasant fashion, as though this was a new experience for him, being in contact with the naked body of an attractive woman. It was crazy and comic, and could prove embarrassing. Each time she moved, adjusting her position on the narrow piece of rock, the additional pressure appeared to become more deliberate. And Enid Porter knew precisely what she was doing.

It was likely to be entertaining, having her as his neighbour on that secluded little bay. And she was not going to be too subtle about it, he thought. Whenever he caught her eye she was smiling at him, and he knew that if he slid an arm around her and kissed her then and there she would not be insulted.

'If you get bored,' she said, 'you can drop by later on, for a drink, I don't usually bother much about lunch, but I might rustle up a sandwich, okay?'

'I'd like that,' he said.

She put on her white cap, patted him lightly on his knee, stood up and took off in a neat shallow dive. He resisted the impulse to go in after her and make a race of it; on his current form she would probably beat him, and he didn't think he wanted that. So he sat on the rock and watched her swim back, her slender arms rising and falling in the morning sun. She was the outdoors liberated lady, lots of fun all round, and ready for almost anything.

She reached the beach and without looking back because she would be sure he was watching her she walked up the sand, her cap swinging from her hand and her hair shaken free. Her bungalow was a replica of his, with pale yellow walls and a steep green-tiled roof, and the usual verandah. The third bungalow was nearly out of sight, hidden by the bushes at the end of the bay where the miniature cliffs began.

David swam slowly back across the bay. His original intention had been to spend most of the day at the table he was going to use as a desk. He was going to sketch out a skeleton of the story he was going to write. He would work all day, and then stroll round to have his main meal in the restaurant in the Reef Hotel. And that was going to be his daily habit. Regularity would be the thing – so many productive hours each day, cut off from time-wasting interruptions and other distractions. Monastic, almost.

The plumbing in the bungalows was excellent, and they were supplied with electricity from the generator at the main holiday complex, all of which made the rents fairly high for the remote location and shortage of vacation facilities.

He took a freshwater shower, and put on

clean slacks and a clean shirt. He had arranged for a domestic helper from the Reef Hotel staff to call in every other day to tidy the place and collect any laundry he might have; so far there had been no sign of her, but after all this was really his first full day at the bungalow, so she would possibly leave it until tomorrow.

He sat at the desk, rolled paper into the typewriter, and stared at the virgin sheet. His mind became a complete blank. He had brought some books with him, including a dictionary and an abridged Roget's *Thesaurus* for which he did not appear to be having much use so far. There were also some paperbacks, and with them John Updike's *Couples*, which he had been intending to read.

He started to read it, and it was so right and beyond anything he could ever hope to produce, it depressed him. Accordingly, when he walked along the beach to visit Enid Porter he had to admit that once again he had achieved just nothing. So what the hell, there would be other days.

She was waiting for him on her verandah; she wore rust-coloured tailored shorts and a loose striped blouse, and as she moved to greet him he knew her breasts were free of any constraint; she looked like a vivacious young woman of twenty-five or so, who was still finding life an enjoyable game. On the verandah there were two deep lounging chairs with bright cushions and foot-rests.

'Are you ready to eat?' she said. 'Settle yourself in one of those and I'll toss out the fodder.'

'You've talked me into it,' he said.

She went inside, and he sat and looked out over the beach to those rocks at the edge of the bay; ever since he had made the acquaintance of Enid Porter, the sexy divorcée from Seattle, the morning had been active. He thought he had a reasonably clear idea of how this acquaintance might develop, and the prospect did not alarm him unduly. She seemed to have no ties, and he could think of nobody who had any claim on him either.

He could hear her humming as she moved around inside the bungalow, and it was a nice domestic sound, normal, it suggested that she had a contented disposition, and that made a difference in any woman, she wasn't so likely to be bitchy. He hoped he was right about her.

She wheeled a loaded trolley out to the verandah. There was coffee, a selection of sandwiches attractively set out, all the right fixings for a salad, a cheese board, and some baskets with a colourful assortment of fruit. Whatever other talents Enid Porter might have, she was certainly no novice about kitchen chores.

'For a lady who insists she never bothers

much about lunch,' he said, 'you do pretty well–'

She smiled and manoeuvred the trolley between the two chairs. 'Think nothing of it,' she said lightly. 'When I finished high school, and that was longer ago than I like to admit, I worked in the hotel and catering business for a while, I can run a restaurant or a bar with the best of them. Then I kind of drifted into show business, I was a cabaret magician's assistant, you know the kind of thing – fishnet tights and boobs on show whenever I stooped; I even did a stint as a stripper when the going got tough – you name it and I guess I've done it sometime or other.'

She poured coffee for both of them. She took hers black and unsweetened, and with it she had a scooped-out grapefruit, nothing else.

'If you think I need nourishment,' she said, 'you can buy me dinner at the Reef Hotel tonight, the food's okay, I drop in there most nights.'

'It's a date,' he said. He had started on the sandwiches, they were crab, which he usually avoided, but these tasted particularly good, and the coffee was the best he'd had for a long time.

'What line of business are you in, David?' she asked.

'Property,' he said. 'Industrial development projects, that's our field in the broadest sense, and we have associates and allied interests all over the place.'

'Big,' she said.

'Quite,' he agreed.

'The label is multi-national, correct?'

He smiled. 'A fairly loose expression, I always think. The company policy is to diversify our interests, and our shareholders like to see a profit.'

'Who doesn't?' She was glancing past him. She said one unladylike word, then got up quickly. 'Excuse me a moment.'

She hurried off the verandah and along the path. A young man in a flapping white shirt and faded khaki shorts had emerged into the sunshine; he had a muscular body and thick dark hair, and he was scowling as Enid approached.

She caught his arm and swung him round to make him walk back the way he had come, and he was clearly unwilling to go. He shook Enid off and stared back at the verandah. David could hear their voices – the young man's angry and Enid persuading, coaxing him. Obviously an argument was in progress, and the man was refusing to do what Enid wanted.

She might be needing some assistance, so David stepped down off the verandah. She saw him, waved him quickly away and once more caught hold of the rebellious young man. This time she made him move back towards the path into the trees and out of sight. David waited there for a few moments, wondering if he ought to follow them. It was evident that Enid and the man had not been strangers. It was also evident that the man had been upset at the sight of David on Enid's verandah.

Enid said that she had been doing that swim across the bay every day for over a month, so she would certainly have aroused keen interest in most of the males on the Reef. That made sense.

David went back and poured himself more coffee, and took care of more of the sandwiches, chicken this time. He was dealing with the cheese when she returned.

She came up on the verandah, her face composed, and her voice was unemotional as she said, 'Sorry about that, he's just a local lad who gets a bit out of line sometimes, no harm in him ... he thought I was going sailing with him, it must have been a mistake, or it quite slipped my memory. That was Pat Quiney, he's a lot of laughs normally...'

'But not this afternoon,' said David. 'He sounded to me like a very angry and disappointed young man who was in love with you and didn't like to see me sitting here. In fact at one time I thought I might have to ride across the sand and rescue you. Only discretion restrained me.'

She smiled mischievously. 'That figures.' She selected a peach from the fruit basket, looked at it without interest and put it back. 'Like I said, Pat's only a kid, but he can act pretty physical at times. I can handle him.'

'I'm sure you can.'

Her smile widened. 'The way you said that, it might be kind of insulting.'

'Listen,' he said, 'all I mean is that you are a lady of character and sophistication, and that I can well understand how you have to brush off the importunate males like Pat Quiney—'

'He's eighteen years old,' she said, 'and that's not my fault, he hangs around and I don't like to slap him down too hard. I know, I'm old enough to be his mother, but he doesn't act much like a son.'

'So he's a normal healthy young man,' said David.

She picked up a small leather case from the trolley. It held some miniature cigars, thin and pale brown, and she offered the case to David. He shook his head and smiled. There were matches on the trolley, and while she fitted a cigar into a little amber holder he had a light ready for her.

'I gave them up years ago,' he said, 'but I'm still tempted.'

Her fingers touched his wrist lightly, steadying the match, but not making a subtle business out of the contact.

'How long do you think you'll be staying here, David?' she asked.

'I haven't decided,' he said. 'I have a long summer vacation and it's just started, the first real break I've had for a couple of years, so I don't plan to hurry back.'

'Good,' she said. After a while she got up and wheeled the trolley back into the bungalow; he offered to help with the washing up but she said it wasn't necessary, thanks very much. She would take care of it later.

When she returned she sat on the verandah railings, one slender leg swinging free. Framed against the sunlit beach and the sea, she might have been posing for an illustration in a holiday brochure, and there was a thoughtful expression on her face. A secret sort of woman, he was thinking – her life so far would probably make the basis of a goodish story. She was the kind of sexy woman around whom things happened. Men.

He stood up. 'Thanks for the lunch, what time shall I collect you tonight for dinner?'

'About sunset,' she said. 'I mix a pretty fair martini, or I can offer you a genuine bottle of real Scotch, Bell's – that do?'

'Beautiful,' he said. He was looking at her as he said it, one short step forward and he could have had her off that railing and into his arms, he was sure. And he didn't think she would slap him in the mouth. She had tipped her head on one side, waiting, with just a touch of amusement in her eyes.

He went down the two steps to the path and it was too late, and when he glanced back she had gone inside the bungalow.

It was early afternoon and the heat was well up. There was no breeze now off the sea. He had no kind of air-conditioning in the bungalow, only a small electric fan that stirred the air around a little but mostly in its immediate neighbourhood. He stripped to his pants and bullied himself into sitting at the typewriter. He did some erratic practice lines – the quick brown fox jumped over the lazy dog all down half a page. The lower-case c was sticking and he poked at the workings with the blade of a knife.

He looked out of the window, and there was a small dinghy with a brown sail almost across the bay. There was very little air moving, and the dinghy was making slow progress. He recognised the young man at the helm. Pat Quiney, bare-chested, hairy and obviously loaded with muscle. The dinghy finally made it to the beach, the sail came down, Pat Quiney hauled the craft clear of the water, picked up a shirt but didn't put it on as he went up the beach to Enid's bungalow.

David could see part of Enid's bungalow,

one end of the verandah, but not the door. Pat Quiney had gone inside, and David waited to see him being evicted. Or maybe they'd both appear and Enid would go for that sail she said she had forgotten about.

Nothing happened. The dinghy remained on the beach. The sea-birds wheeled and squawked about the bay, and the tide dragged up and down on the beach. An hour passed and nobody came out of Enid's bungalow. There was nothing untoward taking place as far as David could see, and he had moved out to sit on his verandah where there was rather a better view.

His imagination was beginning to conjure up some explicit and disturbing pictures about what might be going on over there. If that hunk of beefcake, Pat Quiney, was being 'physical', as Enid had put it, then perhaps she might be needing help without being able to call for it. And then again, she might not be a victim – she might be an active participant.

He could walk along there and barge in and be an embarrassment to everybody, including himself. He had known Enid just a few hours, he had to admit that he was attracted to her, and he had thought the attraction might be mutual. So the thought of her perhaps in bed with young Quiney was less than welcome. It was her business entirely, of course. If she was promiscuous it had nothing to do with him. It was a pity, though.

Casual bed-hopping had never been one of his hobbies, and since his wife had vacated the scene he had seldom been seriously involved with a woman. In recent years his job had kept him on the move so much, and an unexpected phone call from head office had more than once ruined what might have developed into a pleasant and lasting association. Few women are prepared to cope with a partner who is too long and too often on the other side of the globe.

He cherished the vague expectation that one day it would be different. He was earning plenty of money now, and his place in the firm was good and secure. He knew he was reckoned to be an asset to the firm, with bonuses and stock options he would one day be director material for one of their many undertakings.

The time would come when he would want to put down some roots. He was thirty-six, and he ought to be thinking about a wife and a settled home.

The afternoon was well advanced when he saw Pat Quiney walk down the beach, wearing his shirt now; he had to shove the dinghy out before it was floating, then he got aboard and hoisted the small brown sail.

There seemed to be a little more air moving offshore, and the dinghy dipped and got clear of the bay faster than it had arrived. It rounded the point where the rocks came down to the sea, and was soon out of sight.

Enid Porter remained inside her bungalow. David was hoping that she was all right, and he finally decided that she didn't need him and possibly wouldn't welcome him just yet. It was not an original situation, an attractive and experienced woman with a much younger man. Just sex. It happened all the time.

SIX

He gave up even the pretence of doing anything sensible at his desk. He was not in the mood. If there had been a phone he would have rung Enid and made some excuse for cancelling the dinner date. It was going to be something of a bore now, since he did not intend to compete with a young stallion like Pat Quiney for the favours of Enid Porter, of whom he knew nothing except that she had an attractive body, an oncoming manner and no current husband. She was also expert in the water.

It was not quite sunset; there was a little gentle air moving out off the land, and the sky was tinted with streamers of sun-burnished cloud formations. It was an evening when only pleasant things should be happening, and as he went along the path by the beach he was regretting that he did not feel more festive.

Enid came along the path to meet him; she wore a blue trouser suit and a frilly cream blouse, and she looked quite spectacular; she had one of her small pale cigars in its holder, and he was relieved that he had put on one of his better shirts and a tie.

'Nice man, you're prompt, I like that,' she said, and slipped her hand under his arm.

'And I think you're pretty charming yourself,' he said. 'Should I have done something about making a reservation at the Reef Hotel?'

'No trouble,' she said, 'they always keep a table for me. I eat there every night. Let's have a drink or two.'

She took him into her living-room, the furnishings seemed the same as in his bungalow, but there was a feminine atmosphere about the room, it was also tidier than his, with some bowls of flowers. She had the drinks on the trolley.

'Scotch?' he said.

'Please.'

It was Bell's, and she was generous with it. She had a martini. 'Cheers,' she said.

He raised his glass. 'To your bright eyes and continued good health.'

'You make with the words very nicely,' she said. 'I had a visitor after you left this afternoon, David.'

He tried some of his whisky, and decided to be honest. 'I know,' he said. 'I saw him arrive and I saw him leave, in his little boat, I hope you had no trouble with him.'

'No bother,' she said. 'We argued, that was all – he wanted me to go sailing with him and he didn't like it when I refused.' She paused and gave David a faint smile. 'Can I guess what's in your mind? You think I went to bed with him, don't you?'

'That's a very smooth whisky,' he said. 'As you promised, genuine.'

'Don't be smart, David,' she said, 'please. We spent most of the time he was here chewing the rag about me not wanting to go boating as we had arranged. He didn't believe I had forgotten, and I honestly had, and then when he saw you here – you can imagine what he felt. Sure, he wanted to make love to me, it would have been strange if he hadn't wanted it, he's healthy and I like him, and I haven't always said no.'

'You don't need to tell me any of this,' he said.

'But I want to,' she insisted. 'I don't want you to have the wrong idea, it matters to me. Pat tried it on with me, of course he did, but when he found I wasn't going to let him he stopped. He's never never tried to force himself on me, not really, he doesn't have the nerve, and he knows he'd never get away with it. He's a bit scared of me, I think.'

'He would be,' said David. 'You are a very fascinating lady, and I don't imagine he will have met anybody like you before.'

'I should have stopped it before he got serious,' she said. 'I ought to be ashamed of myself.'

'But you're not,' he said.

'You think I'm a tramp, don't you?'

'I think you're a lovely woman,' he said. 'Vulnerable and generous, and when Pat Quiney is an older and a wiser man I think he will be grateful for having known you.'

She smiled, a little sadly. 'I managed to smooth him down before I got rid of him. He was full of questions about you, but there wasn't much I could tell him, was there? There was a lot of hot and angry talk between us in here, but that was all really, no damage. He behaved just the way I might have expected.'

'The impetuosity of youth,' said David.

'He's really quite a nice boy,' she said, 'and Roker's Reef isn't exactly swarming with unattached males, I'm making excuses for myself, and I shouldn't – I like sex and I'm not in the habit of doing without it for long, is that so shameful?'

'I can only repeat,' he said, 'that I think Pat

Quiney is a very lucky young man, and not many men of my acquaintance would disagree with me.'

'This is one hell of a conversation,' she said. 'Let's have another drink...'

The walk along the beach path was pleasant indeed in the fresh evening air. They had just over a mile to go, there was a shorter route up over the high ground and among the trees, but they decided to keep to the coast path where the surface was better. There was little that could pass for a road on Roker's Reef, and there were very few wheeled vehicles. The Roker who had given his name to the place had been a pirate who had operated profitably along that coast for some years at the end of the seventeenth century when buccaneering was in the fashion.

There was a small natural harbour that had been enlarged by the addition of a jetty where cargo could be unloaded, and where the daily ferry called. It was all done on a small scale – there was a marina beside the harbour, where a few sailing craft were moored. The fishing boats were clustered together inside the harbour. The Reef Hotel, the larger of the two in the place, was situated on the higher ground overlooking the harbour. There was a scattering of buildings running up from the water and spreading out along the hillside, just a few shops. Everything looked temporary, or in need of attention, and David could recall a number of projects that he had checked on behalf of his firm – just the preliminary check that would tell him there was no point in going further because the place was a natural loser, and Roker's Reef he placed in that category. It had nothing special to offer, and it would never compete with the established resorts and holiday spots.

'I suggest we eat and then get out fast,' said Enid as they approached the Reef Hotel. 'Too many creeps around here – and here comes the worst of them...'

Charlie Olestead, who was in general managerial charge of the Hotel and the conglomerate of holiday cabins behind the Hotel, was a middle-aged man, overweight, and with the anxious expression of a man who knows he will be looking for another job pretty soon if things didn't pick up, and he also knew they were not ever going to do that on Roker's Reef.

'Well, well,' he boomed, 'glad to see you two good folk have got together. Good-evening, Enid, and you, sir – I was just sure you would appreciate having such a lovely neighbour...'

'Quite,' said David, and deftly steered Enid out of Charlie Olestead's reach, be-cause it had clearly been Charlie's intention to take Enid's arm and conduct her through the restaurant to her table.

'Anything you nice people need,' Charlie announced after them, 'do let me know – I recommend the beef, you will find it super-lative.'

The restaurant was spacious and by no means crowded, and as he followed Enid through the room to her favoured table by the picture window David noted the friendly greetings she was receiving from some of the diners, and he also noted that the male diners appeared more cordial than their companions in some cases, which made good sense since Enid was unfair competition for most of the women there. She was the kind of a woman who would seldom be overlooked in any assembly.

Her table was in the best position for keeping the rest of the room under survey, and Enid looked radiant and poised as she settled herself. She was accustomed to making an entrance, and she had done it again. The head waiter himself was in instant attendance, and he respectfully agreed with them that the beef would be a sound choice.

'There are lots of nice people around here,' said Enid when they were alone for a moment, 'but Charlie Olestead isn't one of them, he's a groper and he can never keep his hands to himself. I had to toss him out of my bungalow the first night I moved in. He's got a wife and a couple of kids, but that doesn't stop him messing about whenever he gets half a chance. He's a randy old billy-goat, which may not be a ladylike expression, but it fits Charlie Olestead. And another thing, if you ever have to pay him for anything, make sure you get a proper receipt – he's a bit forgetful about little details like that and you may find yourself paying twice. Well now, I guess that's enough local dirt for one evening…'

The meal was good and the service outstanding. They had all but finished when Charlie Olestead was seen to be making towards them.

'Oh God,' said Enid softly, 'the bad smell is back again.'

Charlie halted by their table and beamed. 'I see you enjoyed your meal, that's good. Mind if I join you for a minute?'

He pulled up a chair without waiting for a reply. 'I have something that might interest you, Mr Firth. I'm organising a deep-sea fishing trip with a small group of sportsmen, carefully selected of course, all good sports, we'll be going for marlin and tuna, we're famous all along this coast for tuna, if you've never done any deep-sea fishing before you'll find it a real experience. I promise you – I thought you might like to join us, and I'd be happy to arrange it.'

'Very kind of you,' said David. 'But I've

done some of the deep-sea stuff in the Bahamas, and I didn't find it all that fascinating – I got seasick.'

Charlie Olestead smiled. 'Too bad, if you change your mind before the end of the week I can still fix you in. I gather that you are a much-travelled man, Mr Firth.'

'My job takes me around here and there,' said David.

'An exciting and strenuous life,' said Charlie.

'It has its moments,' said David.

Enid stood up. 'Excuse me,' she said, 'I have to powder my nose, I'll meet you in the foyer, David.'

Both men watched her cross the room, and as they sat again Charlie said, 'a lovely woman, and deservedly popular around here.'

'Yes,' said David.

'We don't get many visitors here from your part of the world, Mr Firth,' said Charlie. 'We're a bit off the map. I understand from your secretary in Vancouver that you work for Bastable Walker.'

'I do,' said David.

'That's a very powerful organisation.'

'It is,' said David. 'We have connections all over the place.'

'I'm flattered you found your way here,' said Charlie.

'A long delayed vacation. I'm here for

peace and relaxation.'

Charlie smiled. 'You have my guarantee, Mr Firth – you won't find anywhere along this coast so peaceful and relaxing.'

'Good,' said David. He caught the waiter's eye and took out his wallet.

'Put it away, please,' said Charlie. 'It's on the house.'

'Thank you,' said David, 'but I prefer to pay. I know how it is in the entertainment business – you'll find better uses for your expense account, right?'

Charles wondered if he was being put in his place, maybe there was the insulting suggestion that he fiddled his expenses and a smart executive like Firth would know.

'If it would be more convenient for you Mr Firth, you could settle up weekly … you'll be having a number of meals here.'

'I'll pay as I go,' said David. Charlie watched him settle the bill, and noted the impressive tip he had left on the plate. Charlie began to work himself into a worried state of mind. There were too many puzzling items.

Such as: David Firth who worked for an organisation with world-wide connections had chosen Roker's Reef to spend a vacation where he said he needed peace and relaxation – on Roker's Reef, of all places. With his contacts he could have got in anywhere in the super-plushy spots. It didn't make too much sense.

Charlie's habitual uneasiness, and his persistent belief that the roof would fall in on him one day soon, became suddenly more acute, upsetting his stomach. This Firth character could mean bad news. He was too smooth and tricky.

David Firth stood up, smiling like a satisfied customer. 'A very good meal,' he said, 'we'll come again. Incidentally, include me out on the fishing trip, but thanks for the offer. I do hope you and your sporting chums have a jolly day out on the briny.'

Charlie guessed he was being made fun of by this sarcastic whizz-kid.

'I just wanted to make sure you had a pleasant vacation,' he said stiffly, 'after you took the trouble to come all this way.'

'It wasn't much of a journey,' said David genially. 'I've been dodging around the North American Continent for some months now, looking at this and that, I was practically on your doorstep.'

'So have a nice time,' said Charlie.

David nodded, and they both exchanged pseudo smiles that meant nothing at all to either of them.

Charlie hung around the foyer until he was sure David Firth and Enid Porter had left his premises, and he didn't reckon they would be sleeping alone. Not from the way they were acting. Then he withdrew to his office. He locked himself in and tried to get a call through to the mainland, and most nights that was seldom a simple or straightforward operation. He had to wait, and that did not improve his temper. He was interrupted by the cashier with the cash to be stowed in the safe. Lucy was a middle-aged spinster, with thin legs and a flat chest and very little in the way of feminine charm, but she was efficient and honest, which Charlie had sometimes found a little awkward.

He had to let her in or she would have stood tapping on the door, and she would have been wondering what he was up to inside there. There was a settee in the office, and Lucy suspected what he used it for when he had some silly girl in there.

He did the cash check with her and the takings were down again. She made sure she had his signature where she needed it, and she stood by while he locked everything in the safe. That always irritated him. She was a frigid bitch, he should have got rid of her long ago, but he suspected that she knew too much – her general attitude made that obvious. The cash discrepancies now and then that he had explained away with his customary glibness, he had been pretty certain sometimes that Lucy wasn't being fooled. She could read a set of figures smartly enough. And the padded invoices that put private cash into Charlie's pocket,

Lucy wouldn't have missed some of them. If she opened her mouth she could mess things up.

So he gave her what he hoped was a pleasant smile. If she had been one of the more amenable females in his employ he might have slipped an arm around her waist, but that would never work with Lucy, she would scream the place down.

'Have you time for a drink with me, Lucy?' he said, and pulled out the bottle of whisky from the drawer of his desk.

'No thank you,' she said primly. 'Goodnight, Mr Olestead.' And out she marched, disapproval in every line of her austere figure.

Bloody woman. Charlie renewed his efforts on the phone. He had to talk to Harry Dollond, because Harry had the biggest stake in Roker's Reef, and if there were going to be any developments Harry would know, and it would only be right for Charlie to know as well. For instance, if Harry Dollond was planning to unload his investment on the Reef, Charlie might find himself dropped in the dirt. Harry Dollond, and his associates, were in the business for a dividend, and Roker's Reef had not shown a real profit for a few seasons, so the chopper had to fall one day soon.

Harry Dollond had a finger in a number of lucrative pies, and he had never encouraged Charlie Olestead to get too nosey about the

Dollond ramifications; he also never liked having Charlie on the phone to him with any business headache except at an arranged time in the civilised middle of the morning.

Dollond had a house in Berkeley, a flat in New York and a ranch near Fresno that he kept as a tax loss. Charlie finally got through to the Berkeley house, and was informed that Harry Dollond was at the ranch. He got the number, he had never been invited to the ranch, which Harry Dollond reserved for his personal friends, among whom Charlie was not numbered.

When he was connected with the ranch he discovered that he had chosen the wrong time; he was breaking in on a poker school, and Harry Dollond was most reluctant to talk to him.

Charlie was suitably apologetic, but insisted that Harry should listen to him.

'I've worked for you for a number of years, Harry,' said Charlie urgently, 'and I wouldn't bother you if I didn't think it was important – tell me on the level, are you planning to dispose of your investment in Roker's Reef? I reckon you owe me a straight answer.'

There was a pause, just long enough for Charlie to think that maybe he had got his boss on the wrong foot and off balance. So he might be getting the truth.

'Is that what you've called me up about,

Charlie? At this time of the night? Where the hell did you get the idea that I'm selling the Reef holding?'

'So it isn't so, then,' said Charlie.

'Hey, Charlie, what's this? Who's been talking to you?'

'Nobody,' said Charlie.

'Goddam,' said Harry Dollond, 'you'd better explain, and you'd better make it good – okay?'

'Well, I didn't think you'd arrange to sell out without letting me know first,' said Charlie. 'Harry have you ever heard of a property firm called Bastable Walker and Associates, from London, England? They seem to have branches all over the place.'

'I've heard of them,' said Harry Dollond. 'Why?'

'One of their men checked in here yesterday, a guy by the name of David Firth, he says he's here on a vacation, but I don't think that's likely, not here.'

'You're knocking the product that pays your wages,' said Harry, 'but I know what you mean.'

'My impression is that he's one of their snoops, and he's a sharp character who'd be worth watching. I've talked to him but he doesn't give much away. He's in the property development business, and I find it interesting that he fetches up here – am I right, Harry?'

'I'll do some checking at this end,' said Harry. 'How long is he staying with you?'

'Probably a month,' said Charlie.

'Keep an eye on him, and I'll send along somebody to support you.'

'I've rented him one of the beach bungalows,' said Charlie. 'I quoted him the top rate and he didn't make a squeak, a bit suspicious in a property man, don't you think, Harry?'

'It won't be his money, probably,' said Harry. 'If he is in fact snooping for an outfit as big as Bastable Walker he'll be loaded. I'm inclined to agree with you, Charlie – it's interesting to have a guy like him fetch up at Roker's Reef.'

'He doesn't want to go fishing,' said Charlie, 'I tried him on that, and he didn't show any interest in what I offered – riding and sailing. But he didn't waste any time getting alongside the woman who has the bungalow next to his – Enid Porter. They had dinner here tonight.'

'That's good,' said Harry. 'So he isn't likely to move off before we know something about him, something more – it may be a waste of time, just keep him occupied and in your sights, Charlie.'

'That shouldn't be difficult, not here,' said Charlie.

'I'll be back in Berkeley tomorrow morning,' said Harry. 'We'll be in touch. What's the cash position with you, Charlie boy?

Those last figures I saw from you were too lousy to be real.'

'Business is bad all round,' said Charlie. 'You know that, Harry, but it'll improve.'

'Maybe selling Roker's Reef would be a good idea after all, know what I mean?' Harry's voice was thoughtful, almost as though speaking to himself.

'You're joking,' said Charlie. 'You got to be joking, Harry.'

'You hear anybody laughing? I don't make jokes about losing money, Charlie.'

'I know,' said Charlie. 'But you're only kidding around, okay?'

'G'-night, Charlie boy – watch yourself.'

'Now listen a minute,' said Charlie, but the dialogue was over, and that hot uneasy spasm was starting up again in Charlie's belly. He told himself, and not for the first time, what a tricky bastard that Harry Dollond was, he'd stick a knife in your back as soon as look at you.

Charlie reached down and took the bottle of whisky from the lower drawer in his desk. He was not by disposition a convivial soul, and in recent years he had done more and more of his serious drinking alone, as now. The liquor put him in an ugly mood, and he wanted a woman; his wife would be asleep in the chalet behind the main building and she wouldn't want to let him have it, not without a lot of hassle and bitching, like she always did when he'd had a few drinks and wanted a bit of loving; it would never be worth the bother.

He tried to think of one or two women who might be available, and the choice was limited indeed; attractive and unaccompanied women did not exactly flock to Roker's Reef; Enid Porter was an exception, and look what a disappointment she turned out to be – Charlie could still remember the wicked impact of her knee into his groin when she bundled him out onto the verandah … and it had taken him half the night to crawl home.

There was Ruby Fawcet in her bed and breakfast dump down by the water; she would expect payment because her business was slack like everybody else's business. She was a good lay. But Charlie never liked paying for it. So he sat there and went on with the whisky, so that eventually he knew he was just about beyond doing anything with a woman, even a sexpot – and there were none of those around.

They halted by her verandah. 'Thank you for a lovely evening, David,' she said. 'It was fun and I enjoyed it.'

'Good,' he said.

He had an arm around her waist, and she was allowing herself to lean gently against him, which he found delightful.

'It's been a long day and quite exciting,' she said.

'And it started out there on those rocks,' he said. 'Are we going swimming together tomorrow morning?'

'I'd like that. You call for me, David, not too early.'

He turned her into his embrace, and held her with a spread hand covering the curves where her hips began. He could feel the gentle movement of her breathing against him, and when she laced her hands together around his neck her breasts were thrusting at him and in the starlight her eyes were bright.

So he made his embrace far more enveloping in a manner that could well have taken her off her feet, and together they began the kind of kiss that should rightly culminate in only one way. It was intense and whole-hearted on both sides, and it was Enid who had to end it because her head was swimming and she was having trouble with her breathing.

'David, David,' she said softly, 'that was really something…'

'You're enchanting,' he said. 'You're intoxicating. You're beautiful – are you listening to me, darling Enid?'

'I can't hear anything else,' she said.

He had pulled her back into his arms now, and he held her fast.

'I want to make love to you,' he said.

'I know,' she whispered, and with the tips of her fingers she softly stroked his cheek. 'Will you be angry with me if I say I think we should wait until we know each other better?'

'I can wait,' he said, 'but not too long, please...'

'You're so nice,' she said. 'I'm not a tease, David – it's just that I think we shouldn't rush things... I'd love to have you stay with me tonight, but I wouldn't want you to wake up tomorrow morning in my bed and perhaps wonder what you had let yourself in for – we've both been on this merry-go-round before. Does that sound dumb to you?'

'No,' he said.

'You're not angry with me? You don't think I'm putting on an act and playing hard to get?'

He smiled and took hold of her gently by her shoulders, and she stood with her arms loose at her sides, waiting, submissive, and very lovely.

'Now listen,' he said, 'this is important – you were quite right to treat me with caution, I was taking too much for granted–'

'We both know the score,' she said. 'We have both been scorched in the past – but I can't pretend I don't want to have you with me–'

'And that will have to do for the moment,'

he said. 'Sleep well, lovely one, I'll call for you in the morning.'

He took his hands away from her, and she thought he was going to kiss her again.

'Good-night, David,' she said.

'Good-night,' he repeated softly. 'You'd better go in now.'

She climbed the short step up to her verandah, and when she looked back he was already walking along the path that skirted the beach.

SEVEN

He had almost reached his bungalow when he noticed the shadowy figure of a man down there on the beach, motionless, apparently just watching him. During their stroll back they had met nobody once they had left the road to get onto the coast path. They had seen the lights of a ship out at sea, heading down the coast, otherwise their slice of Roker's Reef had been their own private property. Until now.

David stood for a moment by his bungalow, staring hard down at the figure on the beach, and by now he was sure it was Pat Quiney, wearing some kind of a light jersey or shirt and dark slacks; standing immobile in the sand.

The notion that Quiney might have been spying on them filled him with a quick spurt of anger. There was a light over the verandah, so he went up and switched it on. Then he planted himself full in the light and stood facing the beach.

It was an open invitation to Pat Quiney to come forward. He needed sorting out, and David felt he was just in the right mood to do it. Nothing happened. Quiney did not move. It was a crazy situation, and David decided to sit on the railings of the verandah and wait it out.

Then Quiney began to shuffle over the sand towards him, and when he had come into the verandah light David could see his face, very tight and hostile. His muscular shoulders were hunched, and there was nothing at all friendly about his appearance.

He halted below the steps of the verandah and glared up at David. 'You fancy yourself, don't you?' he said. 'You don't look anything special to me, mister.'

'That's a bit of a primitive approach,' said David.

'So what do you aim to do about it?' said Quiney, and his tone could not have been more insulting.

'That sounds like an old-fashioned challenge,' said David, 'and we both know what this is all in aid of, don't we?'

'I don't much like you, mister – isn't that enough to get you started? Why don't you clear off back where you came from before something nasty happens to you? Nobody around here needs you.'

'That's schoolboy talk,' said David, smiling. 'You should have grown out of that stuff by now, you're a big boy, why, you're nearly grown up.'

Pat Quiney took a deep and noisy breath. 'You're asking for it,' he said and his voice was thick with feeling. 'I'll have to give it to you right now!'

'My, my,' said David, 'you talk rough sometimes.'

Quiney came up onto the verandah in a rush, jumping the steps from the sand, and swung with his right fist at David's head. If it had connected the encounter would have come to a speedy conclusion. But the punch missed wildly because David had shifted just enough to slide away from it. When Quiney tried to follow up with his left he fetched up against the bungalow door, quite violently.

There was too little room on the verandah to make it a suitable battle area, and David reckoned he had pushed his luck about as far as it would go.

Quiney was young and fit, and he was getting very angry at the way the engagement had gone so far. His chest was heaving and his shirt had come adrift from his slacks.

'Why in hell don't you stand and fight like a man?' he said.

David smiled, inoffensively he hoped. 'Why don't we talk this matter over? Wouldn't that be sensible?'

'Scared already?' said Quiney contemptuously. And he made his next assault with more caution than before; he connected with a long looping left that made David feel he had lost at least the whole of one ear. So while Quiney was winding himself up to deliver a devastating clout with his right fist, David ducked inside, butted Quiney in the face and kneed him viciously in the groin. Quiney's face came down in agony, and this time David butted him hard in the mouth. It was all executed quickly, and it was effective and brutal.

Quiney slid down onto his knees, and David pushed him down so that his face was on the floor. Then David planted his knee in the small of Quiney's back and yanked his head back by tugging at his hair.

'Is that enough for you?' he said.

Pat Quiney grunted and slapped impotently with his hands on the floor like a defeated wrestler.

David got up and stood clear. Quiney rolled over and sat up, carefully and painfully. His mouth was bleeding and the front of his shirt was stained with his own blood. He was clearly a most unhappy young man.

'You're a dirty fighter,' he said, tenderly fingering his lacerated mouth.

'I served a spell in the British Army,' said David. 'Unarmed combat is not unheard of over there – you were in a hurry to demolish me, so I had to do something... I'm sorry if I was too rough for you.'

Pat Quiney cleared his throat, but said nothing intelligible, and he remained sitting on the floor.

'I don't think Mrs Enid Porter would be too pleased to hear that you and I have been involved in a vulgar brawl over her,' said David.

'Are you going to tell her?' said Quiney.

'Is there any reason why I should?' said David. 'But I have to tell you this – I don't like the idea of you following us around, snooping, like tonight. There won't be any more of that, understood?'

Quiney looked up at him sullenly. 'I don't take orders from you. I'm in love with her, and you'd better believe that, mister. Maybe it's a joke to you, but it's the most serious thing that ever happened to me. Everything was great, and then you had to come along and mess it up – so I'm jealous, and I hate your guts, and I'm telling you to clear off back where you came from.'

As he finished he stood up, but not quite

straight because of the ache in his groin. He had lost the opening skirmish, but he was nearly ready to continue the conflict.

David held up one hand. 'Now listen,' he said, 'Mrs Porter is a free woman, and as far as I know she doesn't have to ask your permission for anything she wants to do. Furthermore, I intend to stay here on Roker's Reef just as long as it suits me, and if the lady likes my company that will be fine – and you can forget your heavy breathing act. I don't want to have to fight you every time I meet you, it's just too crazy, don't you think?'

Quiney shuffled over towards the verandah steps.

'If you upset her,' he said, 'if you make her unhappy I'll come after you, mister – and if it's bad I'll probably kill you, in spite of your fancy tricks, so you'd better keep that in mind. My advice to you is get on that ferry pretty soon–'

'I understand your position,' said David politely. 'Now forget the feud and come in and let's have a drink.'

'Stuff your drink.'

'Well at least come in and clean yourself up, you can't go home like that,' said David.

'I'll go home any goddam way I please.' Pat Quiney went down the steps and round the bungalow and out of sight.

David felt no elation about the way he had

been obliged to handle the young man. He could well understand his feelings – he was crazily in love with an experienced and seductive woman like Enid Porter. Almost certainly he had been making love to her whenever he got the chance. Then along comes an intruder to spoil the scenario, and beat the young lover in a fist fight. Very galling.

Pat Quiney's misfortunes for the night were by no means over. He had plodded homewards in a very distressed condition, with a multiplicity of aches, and dried blood smeared over his shirt. His aim was to get home without meeting anybody. He had almost reached the last of the street lights before the little road that went up to Aunt Emmie's store, when the Reef's one and only police patrol car overtook him and stopped beside him.

Sergeant Halloran was driving, as usual; he treated the car largely as his own private transport, and members of his tiny staff seldom were allowed to use it, except in a dire emergency, such as when Halloran was sick or off the Reef.

He was a big man, and he had been passed over too often for promotion. He was moody and unpredictable, and now he was just hanging on for his pension.

Abie Garrett was in the passenger's seat,

and as soon as the car stopped Abie was out and doing his constabulary bit in front of his Sergeant.

'This is the feller,' he said, towing Pat Quiney over to the car. 'This is the feller I been telling you about, Serge – Pat Quiney. Always creeping around at night ... look at him–'

The Sergeant got out of the car without haste. He inspected Pat Quiney.

'You been fighting, boy?'

'Just a little disagreement,' said Pat. 'Nothing serious, Sergeant–'

'Who was the other guy?'

'I'd sooner not say, on account of he beat me,' said Pat hesitantly. 'I mean, I thought I could handle him okay, but he really sent me to the cleaners – he was off a ship, down at the docks, and we had this argument over a girl...'

Abie Garrett sniggered; he was not at all unhappy at the thought of Pat Quiney getting himself roughed up down on the docks.

'You're a mess,' said Sergeant Halloran. 'Your Aunt Emmie is a respectable lady, what is she going to think when she sees you like this? You ought to be ashamed of yourself.'

Pat Quiney nodded.

'And over some waterfront floozie,' said the Sergeant. 'You ought to spend the night in the lock-up, sonny. Do you good.'

'Let's take him in for questioning anyway,' said Abie. 'I think he's a liar, Sergeant – let's take him in and sweat it out of him.'

'You telling me my job now?' Sergeant Halloran gave Abie a very superior look, then turned to Pat Quiney, gave him the regulation flat stare and said, 'You telling me the truth, sonny?'

'Yes,' said Pat, eagerly. 'I told you what happened, honest...'

'It's time you grew up,' said Halloran ponderously. 'You don't want to end up in the slammer, do you?'

'Oh no, Sergeant,' said Pat, and there was real sincerity in his voice. He was going to get away with it.

'You try staying at home like a sensible feller,' said Halloran. 'You leave those dock-side whores alone, you hear me? Now beat it.'

Pat Quiney took off up the road very thankfully. His luck was changing.

'I still think we should have booked him,' said Abie.

'I recognise the truth when I hear it,' said Sergeant Halloran. 'That's why I'm a Sergeant, Abie. Are you giving me more argument?'

They got back into the car, and Halloran drove down to the waterfront. He seldom did any night duty now, and this trip would make up his quota for the month. He parked by the docks and sent Abie off to sniff around. It might be interesting to see this sailor who had given young Quiney such a rough time. Abie didn't pick up anything, nobody had seen anything untoward down there, or heard anything of a punch-up. In short, the dockside citizens offered Abie no help at all, which was about normal.

Pat Quiney felt pleased with himself. There had been a hairy moment back there when he thought he was going to be tossed into a police cell, but he had kept his nerve and made a fool out of Sergeant Halloran. Very smart.

Now he had to slip into the house, clean himself up in the bathroom and lose the bloodstained shirt. Aunt Emmie would be asleep.

She emerged from her room in time to intercept him before he reached the bathroom, and her reaction at the sight of him was as expected.

'Dear God,' she whispered, 'what in the world has happened to you, Pat?'

'It's okay,' he said, 'it's nothing much, Auntie– I know it looks bad, but I'm really all right–'

'Indeed you're not,' she said. 'You've been fighting, I'm not an old fool.'

She conducted him into the bathroom and made him sit on the stool by the basin, and she made him strip off his shirt.

'You're a wild one, just like your father, so what got you into a fight this time? You're not drunk, which I suppose is something I have to be thankful for...'

She ran water into the basin and found some lint and a bottle of disinfectant.

'There's no need for all this fuss,' he protested. 'I can look after myself, Auntie–'

'I haven't noticed it lately,' she said waspishly. 'You've been behaving like a half-wit, coming in at all hours – and now this. I'm ashamed of you, I'm disappointed in you, Pat, and that's the honest truth – hold still, boy.'

She cleaned him up very efficiently. 'If you were in any serious trouble, you'd tell me, wouldn't you, Pat?'

'I would,' he said. 'This was just a bit of a fight that I got into, it was nothing so terrible–'

'You're mixed up with some girl, aren't you?' said Aunt Emmie. 'Do I know her?'

'No, Auntie,' he said.

'Why don't you bring her here to meet me? I suppose she's a nice girl, isn't she?'

Pat got off the stool. 'Thanks for the medical treatment, Auntie – can we leave the rest of the discussion for another time?'

'I hope nobody saw you coming home in that disgraceful condition,' she said.

'You're not a bit worried about the condition of the other guy,' said Pat from the doorway. 'I may have done homicide for all you know.'

'Any man who fights with you over some silly girl has to be as crazy as you are,' she said. 'Now go to bed and pray for some better sense.'

Early the next morning David had a visitor. She was a round little woman in faded jeans that were too tight for her curves and age group, she had to be at least forty-five or so; she wore a pink blouse, and when she smiled she showed a formidable set of teeth. She was Agnes, a bundle of domestic energy, who had come to tidy the bungalow and attend to any chores that needed doing. She was part-Mexican, cheerful and full of chat.

She had roused him and he hadn't shaved. 'I catch you in bed, Mister Firth – I make you coffee.'

She inspected him frankly, and the large bed that he had clearly occupied alone. And the smile that crept over her brown face was sexy and mischievous.

'Coffee will be fine,' he said. She giggled like a young girl and bounced out. By the time that he had shaved and dressed Agnes had his breakfast ready, coffee, toast and a boiled egg. She had checked the contents of his miniature refrigerator and larder, and had made a list of the basic provisions he would need even for the most elementary housekeeping.

'I bring them later,' she said. 'You pay me when you see me, okay?' She joined him over a cup of coffee, and she drank two cups of her own excellent making while she chatted with automatic fluency, flitting from one topic to another. She peppered him with questions about London and the Queen and the younger members of the Royal Family, and she was manifestly disappointed that he didn't know more about them. She had three children and a husband who didn't work too regularly. She had travelled as far as Chicago once, and she didn't think too much of it.

She did a rapid tour of the bungalow, dusting whatever needed dusting, his type-writer attracted her attention – had he written any books? And he told her not yet.

'You got no wife, Mister Firth?'

'No,' he said.

'You happy like that? Mebbe you don't like women? Mebbe I talking too much.' She grinned at him, flashing those remark-able teeth. 'Mees Porter, she's a nice lady, very pretty.'

'Very pretty indeed,' said David.

'Much better you have a nice lady friend to keep you company,' said Agnes.

'I'm glad you approve,' said David, and his sarcasm was quite lost on Agnes.

131

'You got clothes for washing, I take them now,' said Agnes.

'Good,' said David. He had finished his breakfast, and she made a cheerful and noisy business of washing up. There would be little peace while she was around, but there was no point in trying to shut her up, or snub her. She loaded the laundry bag in the bathroom with the clothes he had left on the floor. She had checked everything, and he was sure that she would have known if he had in fact shared his bed with a woman last night.

'You have yourself a nice time, Mister Firth,' she said when she was ready to leave, 'you hear?'

He slipped a folded five-dollar note into her hand. 'I hear,' he said.

'Anything you want,' she said, 'you let me know next time I come here, okay?' She giggled and ducked her head, and scuttled across the verandah. She went up the path through the trees, following the route Pat Quiney had taken the night before, obviously some kind of a short cut.

The sky was overcast, and the morning was nothing like as sunny as the previous day. He collected his trunks and a towel and walked along to Enid's bungalow. He whistled as he went up to the verandah. She didn't come out. He knocked on the door and let himself in, and he was quiet because she might still

132

be asleep.

Her bedroom door was ajar. He peeped in; the bed had been made and the room still held her fragrance, elusive and delicate. She wasn't in the bathroom or the kitchen. He went back to the verandah and inspected the sea and the rocks, and all he could see of the beach and the rising ground behind.

She had probably gone for a walk, and he wondered how long she had been away from the bungalow. In the kitchen there were a cup and a saucer and a plate on the draining-board, recently used, he thought. In her living-room he noticed a pair of line drawings that were hung on the wall; one of them was a seascape that looked like the bay outside viewed from her verandah, and he thought it was pretty good, the other was a drawing of some trees in a high wind. Both of them carried the initials *EP* in the bottom right corner.

If these were samples of Enid's work she definitely had talent, he concluded, and so far she hadn't mentioned it to him. In her bedroom there was a large portfolio propped against the wall beside her dressing-table. Feeling slightly ashamed of himself, David squatted, undid the fastenings of the port-folio and opened it out onto the carpet. There were some thirty or forty drawings and sketches in the case, some done in charcoal, others in pencil. The standard of work was uneven, but the best he thought original and strong, the product of real skill, a little rough here and there, but genuine.

There were sketches of scenes he couldn't identify, probably Roker's Reef, rocks and cliffs, and the sea. There were some portraits, men and women, a number of them unfinished. Tucked into a flap in the portfolio there were some nudes, and David squatted there and stared for some time at one drawing until he realised that he was looking at a self-portrait of Enid, a full-length reclining figure on one of those lounging-chairs from the verandah. He thought it was a lush drawing, on the verge of being soft porn. It needed colour to do real justice to her, to illustrate the true warmth of her beauty. This surely wasn't a drawing that she would want passed around. He slid it back into the pile with the others, and he told himself that what he was doing was unpardonable.

If Enid liked doing sketches of herself that left nothing to the imagination, that was entirely her own business; she was a woman of experience, and like any other attractive woman she had good reason to be concerned about her own body and its appearance.

He was about to close the folder up when a couple of drawings slipped out. One was a sketch of Pat Quiney, standing and squinting probably at the sun, the beach was suggested in the background; he wore shorts, and he had folded his arms to make his muscles bulge. The sketch had caught something of his brooding challenge to the world. The hell with it all.

The other drawing was very different: Pat Quiney again, nude and posing on the lounging-chair again. He had one leg bent up, and his hands were laced behind his head, and there was a self-conscious grin on his face. There was no coy fig-leaf treatment here, the details were explicit, to show that Quiney was a fully equipped male.

David slid the drawing back, and fastened the folder and arranged it all as he had found it. He was regretting now that he had let his inquisitiveness get the better of him.

She had admitted that she had been to bed with Pat Quiney, and he hadn't thought that terribly depraved of her, in spite of the age difference. He wondered whose idea the nude drawing had been. It wasn't surprising that Quiney fancied himself as the great lover, and as the man in possession he would naturally resent an intruder. Not an original situation, and so far David considered himself a reluctant participant.

Enid was attractive and more than interesting, but David didn't intend to get himself involved in any untidy drama. Last night, when they had strolled back after dinner, and he had kissed her, he would have made love to her immediately with eagerness and, he was sure, a lot of joy. He had reservations now. It might become a messy tangle.

He walked out to the verandah, and saw her wobbling down the path on a bicycle. She waved at him, the bicycle wobbled more erratically, and she dumped it by the railings and took out some parcels from the basket that served as a carrier.

'Morning, David,' she called to him, smiling, 'I hope I haven't kept you waiting too long, I saw Agnes descend on you and I guessed you'd be under siege for a while, so I rode up to the store for a few things. This bike isn't quite my style, I have it on occasional loan from one of the girls at the Hotel. It comes in useful now and then.'

She wore navy-blue slacks and a blue and white striped jersey. She was, he thought, the picture of an attractive woman, at ease with herself and her surroundings. Not at all the kind of woman who might amuse herself doing soft-porn drawings.

'Did you sleep well?' he asked as she joined him on the verandah.

'Always do,' she said. 'Did Agnes make you some splendid coffee and drink most of it herself?'

'She did, and whipped me up a quick breakfast. Does she work here for you?'

'Not too regularly,' said Enid. 'She works, but she likes to talk, and there are times when I can manage without her chat. What did she tell you about me, David?'

'You were not discussed,' he said. 'I'd have stopped her if she had started–'

'Nice of you. I'm afraid I don't have a very good reputation around here, as you can guess. It doesn't keep me awake at night. I used to sun-bathe on the rocks where we met yesterday, starkers, until some of the little sailing boats started running out of wind where they could get a good look at me. One old goat even brought binoculars.'

'Irritating,' said David. 'I'd be surprised if nobody brought a camera. Are we going to swim this morning?'

'Later,' she said. 'Let's give the sun a chance to break through. Sit over there and tell me more about yourself.'

'You know the essentials,' he said. 'I've been separated from my wife for some years, and she doesn't figure in my life any more. There were no children, which was probably a good thing. They would have had a miserable existence – I would never have been at home and I can't imagine Stella doing the caring maternal bit.'

'Stella,' said Enid. 'That's a classy name. What about your family, any brothers or sisters?'

'One sister,' he said, 'younger than me and happily married to a doctor in Edinburgh, a fertile couple – two boys and a girl. All healthy and normal. Whenever I come away after spending any time with them I'm eaten up with envy.'

'It's not too late for you yet, buddie,' she said. 'I never had a kid, there were a couple of near-misses, but I don't like to think of that any more, makes me feel real old and sort of used up–'

'I wouldn't say that's a good description of you,' he said.

'I don't kid myself, not too much,' she said. 'I've been handled too often, and I tell you that as a fact. Are your parents alive?'

'My mother died ten years ago,' he said, 'very suddenly. I was in Western Australia, in the outback, and by the time the message got through to me and I caught a flight back the funeral had taken place. It was a bit of lousy luck. My father is in the antiques and fine-art business, he's a bit of an authority on ceramics and so on. He always hoped I'd join him in the business – he's been successful, but I wasn't interested, not enough to want to spend the rest of my life at it. We didn't quarrel over it.'

'He sounds nice,' she said.

'He's all of that and more, we still enjoy each other's company.'

'I never knew my old man,' she said. 'From all I ever heard he was a bit of a layabout, so I guess he had his problems. When you finished school you didn't join the family firm, what happened to you then – did they throw you out into the cold world to earn your living on your own?'

'Not quite,' he said, grinning. 'I upped and joined the Army, in fact I got myself a short service commission, and for a while I thought seriously of making it my career. It had its attractions, and I liked the idea of being part of a highly trained group of men, disciplined, and all that...'

'The gung-ho stuff,' said Enid. 'You surprise me–'

'I served in Germany,' he said, 'and I did two spells of duty in Ulster – I didn't care for that at all. I hadn't long been married, which complicated things. When my time was up I left and looked for a civilian job, eventually I managed to wangle myself into a minor and quite insignificant spot with my present firm. I found it suited me. I worked, and I moved up the ladder, I contrived not to make too many mistakes that any of my bosses could identify and, all in all, I don't have any complaints – if that makes me sound smug I'm sorry. I'm just a small cog on a very big wheel, enjoying a brief vacation and in some very pleasant company.'

He had been wandering about the room as he talked, then, as though he had just noticed them, he stopped in front of the pair of drawings.

'I like these,' he said, 'especially this one of

the sea, it's very effective. Those initials, E.P., they wouldn't be yours, would they? Did you do these, Enid?'

'I did,' she said. 'I've been fooling around with sketches and drawings ever since I was in high school. It was about the only thing I was any good at. It's just a hobby, David – not important to anybody but me.'

'You don't do yourself justice,' he said. 'These are good, have you any more that I could see?'

'A few,' she said. 'I'll look them out and show them to you sometime, if you're really interested. Let's go for that swim, David. You can change in the bathroom.'

While he got into his trunks in the bathroom, he felt just a little ashamed of himself, and his crafty manoeuvre about those drawings had deservedly misfired, and he told himself that a gentleman would have behaved very differently ... so perhaps after all he was no gentleman. He waited for her out on the verandah; the sun had broken through to some purpose, and the bay was bright and shimmering.

She wore the pale blue one-piece that she had worn the previous morning, and as she emerged into the brilliant sunshine David thought she was as entrancing as any woman he had seen for a long time, with those lovely long legs and the firm high breasts, and the graceful movement that caught the eye and teased the imagination.

Of course Pat Quiney had fallen crazily in love with her, he wouldn't have been normal if he hadn't.

'No racing,' he said when they got down on to the hot sand. 'Just a friendly swim side by side, out to the rocks.'

She smiled and took his hand. 'Okay,' she said. 'I'll keep an eye on you.'

They waded out and then swam together to the rocks. They climbed out of the sea and in a few minutes the sun had dried them. Enid showed David the flattish slab of rock where she used to do her sun-bathing until the fleet of Peeping Toms came on the scene.

'I'm sorry there isn't room for both of us,' she said. 'Do you mind if I hog it for a bit?'

'It's all yours,' he said.

She unslipped her shoulder straps and peeled down the top part of her swimsuit, then arranged herself on the flattest piece of the rock, face down.

'I'll toast myself about ten minutes each side,' she murmured, resting her face on her arm. 'Hell, this rock hasn't got any softer – okay?'

'Very okay.' He watched her for a while, while the sea slapped gently around the rocks. She shifted her head and squinted up at him. She grinned. 'I'm shameless, I know.'

'I can see nothing to be ashamed of,' he said.

'You have the right answers, David. It helps.'

'Mind you don't fry,' he said.

'Not me, I've been doing this for a long time, just a little every day.'

He found himself a reasonable perch on the rock. When she turned on her back he was watching her, and he was finding it difficult to look anywhere else, and consequently he was permitting himself some moments of very pleasant contemplation, to which Enid did not appear to object. Spread out there in the revealing sunshine and naked to her navel, she invited his admiration and when their eyes happened to meet she gave him the private little smile that did not oblige him to feel intrusive or in any way superfluous.

'I can never remember to act like a lady,' she said lazily. 'At least not for long...'

'Feel free,' he said.

She giggled, then she murmured, 'You may be asking for trouble.'

'I look forward to it,' he said. 'Listen, I think we may have company coming this way, I can hear the sound of an engine out there.'

Almost immediately a motor-cruiser came into view around the point beyond the bay, it was following the line of the coast so closely that it would come round the last of the rocks with little to spare. It was an elegant boat, white and blue, probably with cabin and sleeping accommodation for three or four.

Enid replaced her narrow shoulder straps and sat up, and from the expression on her face she did not welcome the intrusion.

'That's Tim Taggart's boat,' she said. 'His sister Vera is usually with him, but I don't see her.'

'Friends of yours?'

'I know them,' she said. 'I knew them back in the States years ago. They've got a place on the cliffs on the other side of the Reef. Tim's a bit of a pill... I'm sorry, David, I'm afraid our nice morning is going to be ruined–'

'There'll be other mornings,' he said. 'I gather this Tim Taggart is not your favourite person.'

She grimaced. 'I could get along without him just now.'

EIGHT

Tim Taggart steered his boat gently towards the end of the rocks, then deftly brought it round and cut the engine. The name *Mucky Duck* decorated the stern. Taggart himself was a heavily built man, middle-aged and well over six feet tall; he had a thick dark moustache that was in sharp contrast to his brown quite bald head; he wore a faded brown shirt and khaki shorts.

'Hi, Enid baby,' he called out, 'I knew I'd find you here.'

'Morning, Tim,' she said. 'Meet David Firth – David, the intrepid mariner is Tim Taggart, and you should never play cards with him.'

Tim Taggart boomed out a resounding laugh. 'Glad to know you, David, don't you ever believe a word that baby tells you about me.'

'How's Vera?' Enid asked.

'Busy,' said Tim. 'A small investment I made last season turned up good, so we are throwing a little party, and you are both invited, as of now.'

'Well, I don't know,' said Enid.

'So what's there to be doubtful about?' said

Tim. 'You've enjoyed our parties before...'

'You mean now?' she said, and she glanced at David. 'What do you think, David? It could be a lot of fun.'

'Why not?' said David. He grinned at Tim and said, 'You're sure I'm invited? I don't know your sister.'

'She'll be happy to see a new face,' said Tim. The *Mucky Duck* had floated tidily in so that it was simple to step aboard from the rocks.

'We'll need some clothes,' said Enid. 'I'm not going to a Taggart party in this outfit, even I don't have that much nerve.'

'Pity,' said Tim. 'You look terrif' to me, baby. I'll ferry you across, okay?'

There was a mooring-place inshore, where the rocks met the cliffs and the beach began; there was an iron staple that had been conveniently driven into the rock, and under Tim's instructions David crawled for'ard and made a line fast around the staple, which meant that they were all able to get ashore without having to paddle. The *Mucky Duck* could swing with the tide but come to no harm in the shallows.

Tim came ashore with them; he had assumed command of the expedition, and as they trudged up the beach he had a masterful hand tucked under Enid's arm. He was the extrovert type, supremely sure of himself, and in that emphatic voice that swamped the conversation he was giving them a run-down on the trip he and Vera had taken in the States, and David had stopped listening before they had reached Enid's bungalow.

Enid took the first shower, and Tim showed how familiar he was with the place by starting to make some coffee, without having to search for anything in the kitchen.

'You aiming to stay here long, David?' he asked.

'A little while,' said David. Everybody seemed to ask him the same question.

'You're a long way from base,' said Tim.

Enid emerged from the bathroom, wearing a short wrap that failed to reach her knees. Tim handed her a cup of coffee and he had no need to ask her if she wanted sugar; he had made coffee for her before. David had managed to sneak a quick glance in through the open door of her bedroom, and he had noticed that the portfolio of drawings was no longer leaning against the wall; there was no sign of it.

While he was standing under the shower David could hear their voices next door, and Enid was laughing, so he guessed she wasn't finding Tim such boring company. When he turned the shower off, their voices seemed to drop to a murmur, as though they realised he could hear them. He fancied he could detect a soft note of intimacy in their murmurings, and he took his time about drying himself and getting dressed. It was probably his dirty imagination working overtime.

He came out into the living-room and found nobody there, Enid's bedroom door was now shut. This was just a bit too blatant, he thought, and decided to move off and leave them to it. They could stuff their party.

Then he saw Tim Taggart, leaning against the verandah railings, his brown pate shining in the sun, grinning at him, as though he knew what had made David look so angry all of a sudden.

'She hasn't run off, David old sport,' he said. 'She won't be long, just fixing her face.' He came into the living-room, his brown hairy legs were more than a little bandy, a horseman's legs.

'More coffee, David?'

'No thanks.'

Tim poured himself another coffee from the pot. 'She's a nice kid, Enid, got a lot of character as well, you only met her a couple of days ago, that right?'

'That's right,' said David.

'She has that effect on most guys,' said Tim.

'I find her very charming,' said David.

'I kind of like the way you said that.' Tim's grin was wide.

Enid appeared. She wore the trouser suit David had seen her in the previous night, but with a cream sleeveless jersey in place of the frilly blouse.

'I wasn't long, was I?' she asked.

'It was worth it,' said Tim. 'So let's navigate.'

Tim steered the *Mucky Duck* along the southern coast of the Reef where the high ground finished in a jagged line of rocks that would be submerged when the tide was full, and he gave the rocks a wide berth. David sat on a folding seat in the cockpit, and now that they had come outside the white water by the rocks Tim let Enid have the wheel, she had evidently steered the cruiser before; occasionally Tim had to have an arm around her waist to steady her and she wasn't minding that at all.

They were making a wide circuit of the Reef, and on the southern promontory, treeless and bare, there was the coastguard station, looking out to the open sea.

'This is a pleasant way to travel,' said David. 'Could you get over to the mainland, Tim?'

'Sure. We came back yesterday evening, no bother. I wouldn't want to do it if the weather looked dirty. I wouldn't call us an ocean-going outfit, not quite, but I've taken Vera down to Fairhaven more than once.

She is a good sailor. We can sleep four with a bit of a squeeze. If you decide to stay here long enough, David, we might fix up a little trip, how about that, Enid? You like?'

'I do,' she said. 'It beats walking, and Vera's the best sea cook I know, it's a miracle what she can rustle up when the *Mucky Duck* is bouncing about.'

After they had been under way for some fifteen minutes, Tim took over the wheel. They had been running close inshore again, and now he was making in towards an inlet that seemed to bend round on itself in a curve, making it sheltered from wind and weather. The sides of the inlet were fairly steep, and the *Mucky Duck's* engine resounded off the cliffs. Tim had reduced speed considerably.

'Bit tricky around here at night,' he said, 'but there's more depth than it looks, some of those old pirate boys used this channel, they'd wrap themselves in round the last bend just ahead of us, and there's a nice sloping bit of a beach where they could run ashore and careen their ships all nice and snug. I have a lease on the place now, the house is up there on the top, you can't see it from here.'

Beyond the last bend, just coming into view, the inlet widened out; there was a stone jetty, and a small building with no windows.

'I keep fuel in there and some tools,' said

Tim. 'I can do running repairs on *Mucky Duck*. It's more convenient than having to hike around to the harbour.'

He brought the boat neatly alongside the jetty, and David helped him to make all secure. There was a rough path that zigzagged to the top. There was a strong marine smell, seaweed and salty pulp.

'I guess the pirates chopped those steps out,' said Tim. 'I had the railings put up, Vera's idea, she's no acrobat she always says, and most of it's kind of steep.' He led the way up and he showed more agility than David expected from a man of his substantial build.

The land shelved at the top into a shallow little pocket, and there was the house in the middle, white and shimmering in the sun, two storeys, stone-built, with a flat roof. There were flowers, stretches of brilliant green turf, and a stand of trees to break the wind in off the sea. A good place to live if you wanted to keep yourself to yourself. A narrow road behind the house climbed up and out of sight over the hill, connecting with the rest of Roker's Reef.

'Lovely in the summer, like now,' said Enid, and waved to the woman who waited for them under the portico in the front of the house.

'We don't hang on once fall starts,' said Tim. 'Vera likes the sun, me too, so we have a little pad in a condominium right there on

150

Key West – sunshine all through the winter.'

'That's the way to live,' said Enid. 'All you need is money, okay?'

Tim laughed his booming laugh, and David didn't feel that he was expected to say anything.

Vera Taggart was a statuesque brunette, matronly in figure, but still of striking appearance. She was probably a few years younger than Tim. She wore a brightly coloured kaftan, and with her vivid make-up and height she had something of the air of a priestess about to perform some Eastern rite.

She glided forward and she and Enid exchanged the regulation theatrical kisses, then she extended a nicely rounded arm to David, and told him how glad she was that he had made it, and he said politely how happy he was to be there. If there was a party toward David and Enid were the only arrivals, and their hostess didn't appear to be expecting anybody else.

This was very much a summer residence, with lofty rooms that were cool against the heat outside. There was a lot of dark Spanish-type furniture, and figured native rugs on the polished floor.

'Okay with everybody if we eat later?' said Tim. 'Let's try a few little potions first, okay?'

There was an array of drinks in a mirror-backed cabinet almost as wide as a piano.

Tim took care of the service, and David noted that Vera drank only lime juice, she was probably on a diet. Tim and Enid shared a jug of martinis, and David played safe with Scotch, although the measure Tim had poured for him could be made to stretch into half an hour of careful attention, and even then leave him feeling reasonably elevated.

'Tim,' said Vera, 'you go put some clothes on yourself, you sure do lower the tone of the place, all those goddam hairy legs...'

'That's my baby,' said Tim cheerfully. 'Hey, David, let's go look the place over, take your drink.'

David obediently followed him out, and Tim began a conducted tour of his property, which David felt was a little superfluous in the circumstances. The house was roomy enough without being any kind of an architectural gem, and much of the furniture in the rooms they visited was rather too showy and heavy for what was meant to be a summer residence; there were few traces of a woman's touch, which surprised David.

Yet there was plenty of evidence of the money Tim had spent on the place; there was piped water and electricity had been brought in from the main supply some three miles away.

'I made them hook us up,' said Tim, 'and put us on the phone as well – and it is about as lousy a phone service as I ever come across. They didn't want to co-operate at first, said we were too far out, but I waved a few dollars in the right direction, know what I mean? So we got hooked up real smart. This place is run by a bunch of dead-beats, I kid you not.'

'It doesn't exactly bustle, not from the little I've seen of it,' said David. 'How do you and your sister get about? I haven't seen much in the way of roads, and you must be some miles distant from the town and so on.'

'I use a beach buggy,' said Tim. 'You can drive it anywhere around here.'

They had reached the garden at the rear of the house, and Tim said conversationally, 'you interested in this – flowers and growing stuff?'

'Not so that you would ever notice,' said David. There was a rustic seat in the corner of the wall that surrounded the garden. 'Let's sit and enjoy the air,' said David, settling himself on the seat. 'This is a nice restful place, if I may be allowed the observation.'

It was pretty clear Tim hadn't dragged him out to admire a very ordinary bit of garden. Tim joined him on the seat, spreading his hairy legs. 'It's okay,' he said.

'Shouldn't you be doing what your sister told you to do, about hiding those legs in some trousers?' said David.

Tim cleared his throat. 'Mind if I ask you something?'

'I don't promise I'll answer,' said David, 'but go ahead and ask.'

'It's about Enid,' said Tim.

'I thought it might be,' said David. 'What's your problem, Mr Taggart?'

'We think a lot of her,' said Tim. 'She's been a friend of ours for a long time, so we feel sort of concerned about her – you can understand that, okay?' Tim shifted on the seat and scratched one hairy expanse of thigh. 'You got that clear?'

'I wonder if I have?' said David politely. 'I'm a guest in your house, otherwise I might be inclined to invite you to mind your own confounded business.'

'Hey, hey,' said Tim hastily, 'let's not boil over, David old sport.'

'Does your sister share your concern for Enid's welfare, or is it peculiar to you alone?' said David. 'Enid is a very attractive woman, we both know that, does your sister consider Enid a potential danger to you? I notice you can hardly keep your hands off her.'

'I knew her before she got her divorce,' said Tim. 'We were more than friends – do I have to spell it out for you? We understand each other, always have done–'

'And now you're warning me off, is that

it?' said David. 'Wouldn't it occur to you that you are just a piece of past history for Enid?'

Tim shook his head. 'I've got her where it matters, and you can take that any way you like, it's a fact.'

'I don't think this conversation reflects too much credit on either of us,' said David, 'so we'd better cut it short. I've known Enid for just a couple of days, I admire her, and as long as I'm here I intend to spend as much time with her as I can. If you don't like it, Mr Taggart, you will have to do the other thing.'

David stood up; he was prepared to quit the scene in a dignified manner, and walk back if he had to.

Tim Taggart stroked his bald head, his heavy shoulders began to shake as laughter rumbled up inside him and then burst forth in his habitual booming fashion.

'Boy, I sure like your style,' he said, looking up at David. 'No hard feelings? Maybe I spoke out of turn–'

'You did,' said David crisply. 'Now can we forget the whole business?'

'Suits me.' Tim stood up and hitched his shorts up over his belly. 'Have you met young Pat Quiney yet?'

'I have,' said David.

'Awkward young bastard,' said Tim.

'He's in love,' said David, 'and that isn't the

case with you or me. He has a good excuse for being awkward – eighteen is a difficult age to fall for a woman like Enid, and that's what has happened to Pat Quiney. She must be good for him, part of his liberal education, I'd say he's lucky.'

'You could be right,' said Tim. 'She's done her best to shake him off, but he sticks around. I've told her to give him the elbow, but she's too soft for her own good sometimes. By the way, I never did hear what line of business you're in, David.'

'I'm with a development organisation, based in London, England. At present I'm here on a long vacation. So what do you do for a crust, Tim? Are you just a well-heeled money baron or do you have to sweat for it like the rest of us?'

Tim's belly jumped up and down with amusement. 'I have a few interests here and there. A London organisation – I wonder if I've heard of them? I get around a bit.'

'Bastable Walker,' said David. 'Head office in London, a number of connections and affiliations around the globe. You may even have made an investment in one of our enterprises.'

'It's possible,' said Tim.

They had started walking back to the house now. Tim touched David's arm. 'Listen,' he said, 'we must have a little talk sometime soon, we might find we could do each other some good one day, you never know, things happen...'

'Indeed they do,' said David.

'Mind you, I always believe in keeping both eyes open for a smart investment,' said Tim. 'If you want to stay in business and keep afloat you can't pass anything up – you have to give it a whirl just in case. Agreed?'

'Right,' said David with becoming gravity.

'You gotta diversify your interests,' Tim announced. 'Watch the percentages – they won't all lose...'

'True,' said David. 'But I'm beginning to think that perhaps you have an exaggerated idea of my position in the firm – I'm just one of the hired boys, you know – you could say that I run top-level errands.'

'I'm not buying any of that,' said Tim. 'You're being cagey, that's okay with me, but I know a promising situation when I fall over one – your head office is way over in London and here you are floating around on Roker's Reef.'

'Strictly on a vacation,' said David.

'Sure, sure,' said Tim, 'same like me, David old sport. I still figure we should get together soon.'

'You flatter me,' said David. 'I assure you, in the firm I work for I carry no weight at all. I just do my best to earn my keep.'

'I respect your caution,' said Tim genially. 'If you ran off at the mouth you wouldn't be much use to your outfit, a heavy organisation like Bastable Walker wouldn't have a gabby character on the payroll, am I right?'

'All the way,' said David, 'and they are not keen on unsolicited publicity, they don't need it.'

Tim smiled slowly and nodded. 'That makes for class, I like it, David, I sure do.'

They went back into the room where they had been drinking; the women were absent; Tim pressed David to have another Scotch, and then went off to change into trousers, as ordered.

While he waited David gave himself a really weak drink; he was wondering when they would be eating; it was some hours now since Agnes had served him with breakfast, and he had been fairly active ever since. It was a strange household, a middle-aged brother and sister living together was a little unusual. Enid had been right about Tim Taggart, he was indeed a pill, devious and pushing. A salesman, selling himself whenever he thought there might be an opening; David had met his breed before – always on the look-out for something easy and profitable.

In the whole of the house Vera's room was the only one with any pretensions to elegance. It was done in pale blue and soft grey, with some thick white rugs, an over-size dressing-table, and lots of mirrors. It had its own small balcony where Vera occasionally did a little sun-bathing – not too much because of her sensitive skin.

Tim's room was on the other side of the bathroom which they shared. Vera would have preferred a bathroom all to herself, but Tim had refused to agree that it would be reasonable. He himself bathed only irregularly, which sometimes in the really hot weather made him sweaty and not pleasant company.

Now Vera was showing Enid some of the recent additions to her extensive wardrobe. She liked parading in front of Enid the kind of clothes Enid would love to wear if she could afford them. Vera's private feelings towards Enid were mixed, she knew Tim would get into bed with Enid whenever he got the chance, and as Tim's sister she disliked thinking of them in bed together, especially when they did it in the house she shared with Tim. He also had some gross habits, like walking into the bathroom naked while she was taking a bath, and expecting her not to mind. Without his clothes he was not a pleasing sight, least of all to a middle-aged sister with practically no sex urges left.

She had draped a set of lounging pyjamas in heavy apricot silk over the end of her bed, and Enid had agreed with her that she had the height and build to carry off that kind of spectacular attire, and they had also agreed that it would look silly on a smaller woman – like Enid, perhaps. Exactly on what occasion Vera might be expected to wear the expensive gear did not come up for discussion.

Then Tim came in through the bathroom, zipping up the trousers he had just got into.

'For God's sake,' said Vera 'you're not in a gent's toilet now, you really should finish your dressing before you come in here–'

'You can quit your bitching,' said Tim. 'You bug me and I have things on my mind.' He cleared a space for himself on the bed and sat down heavily.

'Do be careful,' Vera snapped. 'That's new and I haven't even worn it yet, it cost a lot of money–'

'I know,' he said, 'I paid for it, but I can't imagine when you'll have the chance to climb into it, not on Roker's Reef.'

He glanced across at Enid, and they exchanged smiles privately. Vera and her clothes had been a bit of a joke between them for years.

'Enid, baby,' he said, 'I think we have a prospect in this David Firth – how does he add up to you?'

'I like him,' she said simply.

'Good. He has aroused my interest, so we will do something about him. I need something to occupy me, and this guy who has come all the way here for a vacation could be just what we are looking for. The fact that you like him is going to make it easier–'

'Easier for me?' said Enid. 'Excuse me, Tim, but I don't think I'm with you.'

'Roker's Reef is on the slide, but it has potential if the right moves are made – it could be ripe for a take-over at a rock-bottom price, so suppose this Firth guy has come over here to sniff around for Bastable Walker?'

'I don't think that's likely,' said Enid. 'He's just here on a vacation.'

'That's what he says and he's convinced you,' said Tim, 'which only goes to show that he's no mug.'

'I still think you're all wrong about him,' said Enid.

'But you are going to work on him, all the same,' said Tim flatly, 'and you are going to soften him up – we both know he has a case of the hots for you, in a gentlemanly British fashion – I see no difficulty, baby.'

Vera made an inelegant snorting noise, and started arranging her clothes back into the built-in wardrobe.

'If Firth is here to nose around,' said Tim, 'I want to know – there could be a slice in it for all of us. I aim to see a lot more of this guy – but not as much as you once you get him going. He'll talk to you, baby, and

161

between us we'll squeeze him and he won't ever know it's happening.'

'Tim,' she said slowly, 'I don't like this set-up very much, I don't think I want to go through with it – I have to tell you that right now.'

He smiled, not a very nice smile. 'You're getting out of touch, baby – you know the score, so what's with you now all of a sudden? David Firth won't be hard to handle, not for a performer with your talents and experience.'

'You're making me into a whore, that's what!' she said savagely. 'I'm not going to let it happen any more, I mean that, Tim.'

This time Vera made no attempt to stifle her snorting laugh. She slid the wardrobe door shut with needless vigour.

'You surprise me, Enid,' she said. 'I always thought you enjoyed your work, those intimate bits at least – maybe you're getting a little too old for it–'

'Button it,' said Tim, but there was no real heat in his voice; he and Vera could bicker all day and half the night without having a genuine quarrel, possibly because neither of them listened to the other when it was not convenient.

'Seriously, Enid,' said Vera, 'I've never known you when you weren't on heat for some guy or other – what's this one so special for? If it isn't a dirty answer...?'

'You wouldn't understand,' said Enid. 'He's different, that's all.'

'Now I guess I've heard everything,' said Vera. 'Love's young dream, excuse me while I throw up.'

Tim went over and put his arm around Enid's waist with the casual ease of an established lover. They might have been alone in the room, and Vera watched with a sardonic smile.

'Now, baby,' said Tim soothingly, 'why get yourself into a hassle? We're partners, we always have been – when you're in a jam I'm the one you come to, nothing's changed that.'

'Yuk,' said Vera. 'While you two have a good cry together I'd better go down and entertain our guest, he looks like a perfectly ordinary kind of guy to me.'

'You could be wrong,' said Tim.

'The way I'm feeling,' said Enid, 'I could pack up and leave the Reef on tomorrow's ferry.'

'That wouldn't be the brightest idea you ever had,' said Tim. 'That would foul it up, and I would come after you, which you would not like.'

He had tightened his hold on her and his fingers were spread out over her breast, turning her into his hard embrace. She had to face him, there was nowhere else she could look, and the way he was holding her was having its usual shameful effect on her, weakening her resistance, even when his sister was watching just a few feet away. And he knew it, he always did.

He was showing her that fleshy triumphant grin that she knew so well, and she wished she had the courage to spit in his face.

'It's a bit late to be getting fussy,' said Vera. 'It doesn't suit you—'

'All right,' said Enid wearily.

'That's sensible,' he said. Before he let her go he gave her some extra pressure, folding his arms about her, enveloping her in a blatantly sexual approach, and his grin widened because he was so sure of what he could do to her whenever he chose.

She stared up at him, and her expression was not that of a woman who was about to be seduced. Tim was too carried away by his own potency to notice the way she looked at him.

'That's enough,' she said. 'I've agreed so there's no need to paw me about.'

He released her, he smiled at her and gave her what was intended to be an encouraging pat on the bottom before she moved out of his reach.

'That's my baby,' he said.

Vera laughed silently from the doorway. He just couldn't keep his hands off her, and the sly little bitch was pretending she didn't like it. It was a disgusting exhibition.

Tim was happy. He pointed a jocular finger at Enid. 'When you start working on him he won't know what's hit him – if he's here on some kind of a job for his firm, and I think he is, between us we'll find out, and then maybe I'll pull one of my little miracles and sweet-talk some loot for the three of us.'

'It won't happen,' said Enid. 'This time you're kidding yourself exclusively.'

'You just coax him along,' said Tim. 'You soften him up, it shouldn't be any hardship since you like the guy, you give him the full treatment–'

'Are you telling me what to do?' she interrupted bitterly. 'You know what I think about this business. I'll do it but I don't like it – can't you understand that?'

'Okay, okay,' he said hastily, 'don't go on the boil again.'

'Let's eat,' said Vera.

NINE

Charlie Olestead had a phone call from Harry Dollond who had moved back from his Fresno ranch to his house in Berkeley.

'Now listen good,' said Harry, and from the sound of his voice he was in one of his dynamic Napoleonic moods. 'I'm sending

165

Pinky Slowman over to you, he will arrive at your harbour about three thirty, you be there to look after him – anything he wants he gets pronto, understand, Charlie?'

'Naturally,' said Charlie Olestead. 'I'm glad you're taking this matter seriously, Harry–'

'Of course I'm taking it seriously,' said Harry. 'Only an idiot would take anything to do with Bastable Walker as anything but real serious, and I kid myself I am not an idiot. I'm not sending Pinky to look at the scenery, Charlie – all you have to do is just what he tells you.'

'Naturally,' said Charlie again.

'Charlie boy,' said Harry, 'you sound like you're running out of words, what's the belly-ache this time? You getting nervous?'

'I'm wondering if Pinky is quite the man we need here just now, Harry–'

'You haven't been listening,' said Harry. 'I make the decisions. You do as you're told – you don't even qualify to have any opinion, you're a lousy loss-making manager, okay? Pinky has my backing.'

Charlie found himself about to repeat 'naturally' automatically, when he discovered that the conversation was over. To cut a dialogue short whenever he liked was one of Harry's less endearing habits. He was a pig.

Charlie sat at his desk and thought unhappily about having to work with Pinky

Slowman. The simple truth was that Pinky scared him.

Harry Dollond would deny that he ever used any form of gangster tactics in his business manipulations, or that he ever had occasion to operate on the shadier side of what might be right and proper. Pinky Slowman was officially employed as Harry's personal assistant; he sat in on the conferences and seldom said anything that anyone could remember later. He went on mysterious trips sometimes, and he never reported to anybody but Harry himself. It was thought, with good reason, that Pinky operated as Harry's private hit-man or enforcer, and nobody else in the organisation had ever got near to him as a friend.

In the late thirties, he was slightly built, neat and well-controlled, like a dancer; he had thinning sandy hair, slate-grey eyes, and a florid complexion that had given him his nickname, Pinky. He was a quiet dresser, and could hold a lot of liquor without showing anything for it. He could slide in and out of a fraught situation, leaving no traces of his passing.

Well before the appointed time, Charlie Olestead was down at the waterfront, with the Hotel car; Pinky wouldn't be arriving by any normal route, the ferry had come and gone. A grey cruiser with white trim brought him across the harbour and up to the dock. Pinky was alone and he brought the cruiser smartly alongside the dock steps where Charlie waited.

He threw a line up and Charlie made him fast, then came the luggage, two fair-sized cases. Pinky himself wore a light tweed jacket and beige summer slacks. He joined Charlie on the dock.

'Where's your hotel mooring?' he said.

'Further in,' said Charlie. 'I'll have one of the boys see to your boat. Did you have a good crossing, Pinky?'

'I'm here,' said Pinky. 'Let's get this circus on the road.'

During the short drive up to the Reef Hotel, Pinky said, 'I'm John Brown, don't forget it. John Brown from L.A. I'm interested in conchology, the science of shells and shell-fish, got that?'

'I do know what conchology is,' said Charlie stiffly.

'Clever boy,' said Pinky. 'So if I go wandering along the seashore nobody will be surprised.'

'Smart,' said Charlie.

'Don't get snorty with me,' said Pinky. They went into Charlie's office at the Hotel, and Pinky refused a drink. He settled himself in Charlie's chair at Charlie's desk.

'Now talk,' he said. 'Give me the set-up as you know it. You told a bit to Harry so he sends me here, now I want to hear from you

– make it fast and good.'

Swallowing his resentment, Charlie gave his recital. And throughout it he managed to lay stress on his own shrewdness and mental alacrity in the way he had assessed the significance of David Firth's visit to Roker's Reef.

'I could tell he was no ordinary visitor, soon as I saw him,' he said, 'and after I'd had a couple of talks with him I was pretty sure he would be worth investigating, the same as I told Harry – I'm glad he agreed with me, Pinky, and sent you to chase it up. Did Harry find anything out about Firth's firm, the London mob, Bastable Walker?'

Pinky wagged his head. 'Everybody very cagey. They are big operators, with plenty of clout. You can't guarantee anything would be outside their range. One thing Harry did verify – this Firth guy is reckoned one of their whizz-kids, and he has been moving around in Canada and the States a lot lately, so he should be interesting. I'll move into that empty bungalow on the bay this evening, have it cleaned up and ready for me. I'll eat up here. Now I'll take a little walk around.'

Pinky got up from the desk and strolled out into the Hotel lobby; he was very much the man in control. Charlie sent for Agnes, the itinerant domestic help, and told her to get herself down to the empty bungalow on the bay and make sure it was ready for use immediately. Mr John Brown, a scientific gentleman from the USA, would be moving in that very evening.

After the lunch-party in the Taggart cliff-top residence, Tim Taggart was driving Enid and David back in his beach buggy; it was a much shorter and more convenient journey than cruising round the Reef coast in the *Mucky Duck*. Enid was sitting in the front beside Taggart, and David perched on the rear seat. It was not a comfortable ride, the buggy's springing was hard and the roads were poor.

When they reached the miniature town square, Tim stopped and said he had to collect some shopping for Vera.

'We can walk the rest of the way, can't we David?' said Enid, getting out. 'Thank you for a lovely trip, Tim—'

'But I won't be long,' he said. 'I thought we could arrange another outing.'

'We'll look forward to it,' said Enid, smiling.

'Indeed we will,' said David. He had joined Enid on the pavement. 'Many thanks for the lunch, one evening soon you and your sister must dine with us at the Hotel, okay, Enid?'

'Sure,' she said. 'That'll be fun. See you, Tim.'

Enid had her hand lightly under David's

arm as they strolled off. She had insisted that she hadn't been to bed with David Firth yet, but Tim was sure that would happen very soon, and he hoped Firth would appreciate what a bonus Enid was in bed, even now.

He was so absorbed in watching them that he failed to notice the slender man in a light tweed jacket and summer-weight slacks who was observing him intently from the shelter of a shop awning, and who smoothly disappeared round the nearest corner when Tim Taggart crossed the square to do his shopping.

Pinky Slowman returned to the Reef Hotel a lot faster than he had left it. Charlie Olestead was consoling himself in his office with his private bottle of Scotch, brooding over the unpleasant prospect of having to do what Pinky told him to do. Pinky burst in without knocking, glanced at the bottle that Charlie hadn't been quick enough to slip into his desk and said, 'Still on the sauce, like Harry told me. Boy, you sure are a disaster. Sober up and listen – I've just seen somebody I know, a fat guy with a bald head and a black moustache, driving a buggy–'

'Tim Taggart,' said Charlie, 'that's Tim Taggart, he drives a buggy…'

Pinky straddled a chair. 'Okay, tell me about him.'

'He's got a place on the cliffs, a couple of miles out, lives there with his sister, Vera.

171

They travel around quite a bit, but I wouldn't say they mix a lot here on the Reef, they're not short of a dollar or two, that's for sure. They're occasional customers here, no more than that, and most folk reckon there's a bit of a mystery about them – what's your interest, Pinky?'

'He's a con artist,' said Pinky, 'and he's good, he conned two hundred grand off Harry a couple of years back on a deal they had cooking with some other guys in St Louis. Harry's been busting his gut over it ever since, and he'll be mighty happy to hear we finally caught up with him – he was operating under another name then, he called himself Richard Adam. He skipped out with the cash, a very smooth performance. Like I said, an artist. When I saw him just now he had a woman with him in the buggy, blonde, no chicken, but a looker, sexy shape–'

'That would be Enid Porter,' said Charlie. 'She's in one of the bungalows, she's been here over a month now, Tim Taggart made the booking for her, and she's been visiting them. Where does Vera come into this, Pinky?'

'She's his sister, that's genuine enough. He uses her to make his set-up look respectable. There was a younger feller with them in the buggy, he walked off with the doll – that would be this David Firth, right?'

Charlie nodded. 'He hasn't been wasting any time. He had Enid up to dinner here the night after he arrived–'

'And he's already on friendly terms with the sharper who took Harry for a large slice of loot. So Harry will be very interested to hear that as well.'

'What can be the connection between those two?' said Charlie. 'David Firth is employed by one of the most substantial firms in the business world, he couldn't be mixed up with a crook like Tim Taggart.'

'I wonder what makes you so sure?' said Pinky. He pointed at the phone on Charlie's desk. 'Get me through to Harry's place in Berkeley, and make goddam sure nobody listens in, including you, Charlie boy.'

Pinky then made a brisk tour of some of the Hotel's public rooms, and noted the lack of activity in most of them; he used the toilets behind the cocktail bar and strode back into Charlie's office.

Charlie held the phone out. 'I got through,' he said. 'Harry isn't there, he's on a flight to Chicago, and then New York – you want to leave a message?'

'Skip it,' said Pinky. 'Plenty to do here. You can take me for a ride and show me where this Taggart feller has holed up.'

'My pleasure,' said Charlie thinly. 'Will he recognise you?'

'I don't intend to give him the chance,'

said Pinky. 'Tim Taggart, alias Richard Adam. I'll just take a quick look over the territory.'

'You can get at it by sea as well,' said Charlie. 'They have a private landing-stage, Taggart uses a cruiser pretty often. He can move across to the mainland without being noticed any time he chooses.'

'I will also take a look at that area, in due course,' said Pinky. 'As I said, there's plenty to do here. Bring your binoculars.'

They drove out of Reef Town and within a few minutes Charlie was steering the car along a narrow track that twisted in among the trees. When they emerged into the open he pointed to the little valley that dipped and rose to the cliffs, with the Taggart house under the rise.

'There it is,' he said. He drove a little further along, until there was some cover where he could pull the car off the road.

Pinky Slowman took the binoculars and slipped quickly in among the trees, until he found a spot where he had a clear sight of the house and the garden. And Charlie came after him at his leisure.

For a while there was nothing to be seen but the house in its pleasant position, with the tidy gardens. Tim Taggart had returned because the buggy was standing on the driveway near the rear of the house. Then Vera made a brief appearance, well covered in some kind of a flowing dress, and wearing a broad-brimmed straw hat. She had a basket and she was picking fruit, raspberries.

'What staff do they have?' asked Pinky when Vera had gone in.

'Vera does most of the housekeeping,' said Charlie. 'I've never had a meal there, but she's supposed to be a good cook. A couple of girls cycle in from the town to help out when necessary, and a local feller calls in and sees to the garden.'

'Would you know about it if they had any alarms installed?' said Pinky.

'No,' said Charlie. 'There wouldn't be any local firm that could make a proper job of that. They might have brought in somebody from across the water. You're not intending to break in there, are you, Pinky?'

'Just gathering information.' Pinky gave the area a long inspection, noting obstructions and possible difficulties if he had to make an approach in darkness.

Then he had Charlie drive him back to the Hotel. His luggage had been taken down to the bungalow, and Agnes had returned to report that the place was fit for occupation. She looked for a tip from Pinky, the scientific gentleman. She got nothing.

It was early evening when Charlie took Pinky down the coast path to the bungalow. David Firth and Enid were sitting on her verandah, and they watched the arrival with interest. They had seen the luggage come down and Agnes had told them there was a famous American scientist who would be moving in that evening, a Mr John Brown. Enid had been smoking one of her thin cigars in her amber holder. It had been a tiresome session with Tim and Vera Taggart, and they were relaxing, in the beautiful evening.

They had been expecting an elderly gentleman, probably with thick glasses and a grey beard, and Pinky Slowman came as something of a surprise. Charlie waved at them, and even at that distance they could see that he was fussing over the new tenant, and that he was more than a little nervous.

'He doesn't look much like a scientist to me,' said Enid. 'He reminds me of a guy I did an adagio act with years ago in a Cleveland club, it was a lousy joint and we were not sensational.'

'Scientists come in all shapes and sizes nowadays,' said David. 'I noticed this one didn't have any labels on any of his bags.'

'So he's famous and terribly modest, and doesn't want any publicity.'

'John Brown incognito,' said David. 'I wonder. When Olestead brings him over, and I'm sure he will, we'll have to be polite to him, but not too polite. We don't want him hanging around – is that unanimous?'

'It is,' said Enid. 'Let's take a walk along the beach.'

'I think I'm going to resent the presence of a third party on our bay,' said David. 'It was nice, feeling we had it all to ourselves.'

'We won't let John Brown disturb us,' said Enid. 'We won't let him make the slightest difference to anything we want to do, agreed?'

'Agreed,' he said. 'If he's looking for company he will have a dreary time down here with us.'

She put her hand under his arm, a gesture he found himself liking more and more, and they walked along the beach, past the south end of the little bay, leaving the three bungalows behind them.

Pinky Slowman was unpacking his cases in his bedroom, and Charlie Olestead was looking through the window at David Firth and Enid, strolling in the distance, and Charlie was wishing he was in David Firth's place, with that sexy chick hanging onto his arm and clearly ready to let him have it at the drop of her panties.

In one of his cases Pinky had a small leather container, double-locked. He unlocked it and took out a shoulder holster with its slender strapping; there was a small automatic wrapped in a yellow duster, and a packet of ammunition.

Charlie saw it all as he turned back from

the window, and his face registered instant alarm.

'You won't need any of that here,' he said. 'Not here on Roker's Reef, Pinky–'

'What's this then?' said Pinky. 'Some kind of church? Nobody breaks any rules here, is that what you're telling me? You are not only a lush and a bum as a manager, you are also simple-witted.'

Charlie sat on the bed and stared un-happily at the carpet.

'There hasn't been a shooting on the Reef for years,' he said. 'I don't understand what you need a gun for.'

'You don't understand anything much,' said Pinky. 'There's this operator who calls himself Tim Taggart now, and it so happened that he put the bite on Harry Dollond for two hundred grand – so whatever I do or don't do here, Charlie boy, I aim to deliver Taggart back to Harry and, if I need artillery, I will have it handy. You get the picture?'

Charlie nodded.

'This Taggart is a conman,' Pinky went on, 'and they don't go for guns usually, if there's a showdown they get scared – the same as you would do. I could take this guy from here to Berkeley and I wouldn't have any trouble.'

'So what about the Englishman, Firth? He's not a crook, surely, not working for that firm?'

'Maybe he just keeps bad company,' said Pinky. 'Maybe he is over here just on a vacation, but I wouldn't bet on it. When I put the squeeze on Taggart he'll tell me about Firth.'

Charlie didn't like the sound of any of that, and Pinky laughed at the worried expression on his face.

'You won't have to do anything,' said Pinky. 'I'll take care of it. There is one thing you should know about Harry by now – he does not like having money chiselled off him by some twisting bastard like Richard Adam who now calls himself Tim Taggart. It makes him mad, Charlie, and when Harry gets mad there is calamity for somebody.'

'I know that,' said Charlie. 'I hope he'll remember it's really through me that you made this trip, Pinky. I mean, I called him as soon as I discovered that David Firth worked for Bastable Walker–'

'Okay, so you're smart,' said Pinky drily. 'Listen, before you go back, have somebody make sure my boat has a full tank, and I'll need a map of the Reef, a good chart, I'll pick it up when I come up to eat. Is Taggart likely to be at your place tonight?'

'It's possible,' said Charlie. 'He's not a regular.'

'You watch out for him,' said Pinky. 'I don't want to run into him, he knows me. I'll show up late for food, and if he's there you'd better make sure I know. I'll come in by the staff entrance. If Firth and the chick are in your dining-room, you can introduce me, and don't forget I'm John Brown.'

'I'll remember,' said Charlie. He was dismissed, and as he walked back along the coast path he was regretting that he hadn't turned the job in months ago, because he could see nothing but trouble ahead.

TEN

There was no joy left in life for Pat Quiney. It was all a lousy conspiracy and there was no justice. He had a bad night, and in the morning there was the dried blood on his pillow to prove it. Some of his front teeth had been loosened, and the gums were sore; his mouth was swollen, and when he moved his lips they began to bleed again. Eating and drinking were going to be hell for a while.

He lay in bed and sweated, and he recalled the shameful defeat he'd had. A lot of the guys who knew him around the Reef would never believe he had taken such a quick beating. And the thought that Enid might hear about it had his stomach churning over, she might even find it funny. He desperately hoped that this Firth feller would never tell her.

Aunt Emmie was giving him the frigid treatment, to make him feel he was probably not fit to sit at the same table with her. She relented a little when she saw the trouble he was having when he tried to eat his breakfast. She gave him a straw for his coffee, and a bowl of bread and milk instead of his normal two eggs and three rashers.

'You ought to let Doctor Russell take a look at that mouth,' she said. 'It may be infected. He'll be at his surgery this morning. Did you hear me, Patrick?'

She only used his name in full when she wished to let him know that he might be allowed back into the human race, after some grave misdemeanour.

'Yes, Auntie,' he mumbled. 'If I have time I might do that.'

'You make time,' she told him.

He was not ready to make an appearance in public while he was looking the way he did. He was in no mood to fend off the kind of smart comments he might hear. So he would have to keep well clear of the town and the neighbourhood of the harbour.

There was a job he had been putting off for some time, clearing and tidying a little coppice that belonged to an elderly couple who were trying to sell the cottage they owned along with the coppice. They had moved out, and Pat had already been given a part payment on the job, and he had been feeling guilty because he hadn't even made a start on the job. The Driscolls, the absent owners, were old friends of Aunt Emmie's, and it might restore him to her favour if she knew what he was planning to do.

'I think I'll spend the day clearing that little bit of a wood for the Driscolls,' he said.

'It's about time you got round to it,' said Emmie.

He collected the tools he thought he'd need, including an axe – some vigorous wood-chopping would be good for him, sweat off some energy. Emmie made him some sandwiches and put in a bottle of milk and some straws. She was almost his friendly aunt again.

'Shall I make an appointment for you to see Doctor Russell?' she said.

'I'll wait a bit,' he said. 'I'll see how the day goes – I don't expect it'll be too fatal.' He tried to grin and regretted it because his mouth wasn't ready to oblige, and Aunt Emmie didn't think it was funny either.

The Driscoll's cottage was down on the southern tip of the Reef, and he started off across the fields, avoiding the roads and embarrassing encounters with people who would want to know what the hell had happened to his face. It would take him about an hour, following the paths he had known as a boy. Over some pretty broken ground, and only now and then in sight of a road of any kind. It was already warm and he wasn't hurrying.

He tried not to think of Enid, and he was not successful. She was in his mind all the time, provoking and awakening him, as though he still had her in his arms. He couldn't stand another night without her. He would make her see him, somehow.

His luck temporarily ran out when he reached the lane by the Driscoll place, because down the road came Ossie Sinclair in his father's car. He tooted and stopped, and Pat sat on the grass bank and waited.

'Hiya, stranger,' Ossie called out. 'Where you been hiding, hey?' Then as he came nearer he saw Pat's face. 'Boyohboy,' he said reverently, 'what's the other guy look like, Pat? Is he still living?'

'A minor disagreement,' said Pat. 'Just a skirmish. Nothing to get excited about.'

Ossie settled on the bank beside him. 'I bet there was a chick in it somewhere.'

'No comment,' said Pat loftily.

Ossie rolled himself a cigarette very deftly, lit it and settled back on his arms on the grassy bank, the gold old country gossip posture.

'I'm remembering what Abie Garrett was saying about you in the pub the other night,' he said. 'All this prowling around at night, there can be only one explanation – so who's the chick, Pat? When the cops talk about a guy, that has to be bad–'

'If you want to get your teeth pushed down your throat I might be the boy to do it,' said Pat.

'Always a pal,' said Ossie. 'I do hope you're keeping sober, when you're pie-eyed you're not much use, remember?'

'On your way, Ossie,' said Pat.

'I know,' said Ossie, getting to his feet, 'she's married and her old man caught you at it–'

'You should have been there,' said Pat.

'You young devil, you,' said Ossie. 'We ought to take a run over to Fairhaven one weekend again. Are you doing a job around here?'

'I'm cleaning up the Driscoll plantation.'

'Sooner you than me,' said Ossie. 'It's a wilderness in there, you'll earn your money.'

When Pat got down to the job he found that Ossie had been right – it was a wilderness, tangled and over-grown among the trees, and for most of the morning he was working with a sickle, cutting a way through, and frightening the rabbits. They had been un-disturbed in the coppice for years now, and they were hopping and skittering about in alarm.

He estimated that it would take at least two

full days to make a fair job of it, so he eased off and stopped tearing into the undergrowth like crazy. He had a good rhythm going, and he was forgetting his current problems for minutes at a time. He wouldn't try any tree felling until tomorrow, that would be a serious job.

He forgot his busted mouth until he started to eat his sandwiches, and then it wasn't much fun. Later in the afternoon, when he had pushed the work on really well and he was soaked in sweat, he decided to cool off on the beach and laze around in the sea, it was within a few hundred yards of the Driscoll cottage. He had stripped off his shirt as soon as he had got clear of the undergrowth.

Down below him there was the dirt road that eventually improved and ran into Reef Town itself. He saw the buggy bouncing along, leaving a cloud of dust behind, and he recognised the three people – Tim Taggart driving, Enid beside him, and Firth on the back seat. They were all of a hundred yards away, but he knew them, and the soothing effect of the hard work he had been doing vanished instantly, and he was filled with black rage and envy.

He wanted to charge down there and yank Firth out of the buggy and punch the daylights out of him right there in front of Enid, by God that would be the thing to do.

Instead he sat and punched his fists on the ground, and in his savagery he started his mouth paining all over again. He abandoned the idea of a cooling swim. Nothing was going to make life bearable any more. He was a man apart, and as for Enid sitting in the buggy while that bastard Taggart drove her about and Firth in the back so close that he could touch her – she didn't know he existed any longer.

He lost interest in the wood clearance. Some other time would do.

He had piled up a lot of dried scrub, leaves and branches. He made a heap of everything that would burn and set light to it. It was dark by the time that he had finished, and he had worked out what he was going to do. In the morning he would collect his money from the Reef bank and when the ferry made its return trip to Fairhaven he would be on it. He would be leaving for good, but before he went there was one personal item he would attend to. Then goodbye to Roker's Reef.

He was a man with a purpose. He was also dirty and hungry. Aunt Emmie was out when he got home, and that was okay – she had left food out for him on the kitchen table.

He took a shower and changed into clean clothes. He had a large slice of water-melon, he heated up some soup, and sliced a chicken into tiny pieces so that he could eat them without too much agony. He found the remains of a bowl of custard in the fridge, and spooned it down with noisy relish. He was not going to pass the night in hunger, and it would be wise to have plenty of ballast on board in case some drinking came his way. This would be something of a farewell celebration. And he did not plan to be alone all the time – Enid at least was going to remember his departure.

He walked down into the town later on, and his first call was at the Reef Hotel. There was nobody who interested him in the dining-room, he glanced in the bars and didn't buy a drink. He didn't see Charlie Olestead, which was probably a good thing for Charlie, since Pat was in the mood to pulp the fat bastard if he spoke out of turn.

He made his way down to where the coast path started, and he was just in time to slip under some bushes and squat when they came up the path. She had been laughing, and that had given him the warning. He didn't dare look as they passed, but he was sure he could smell her perfume afterwards. And it made him think of her in her bedroom and the thrill of taking her into his arms, and what would come after ... it must have meant something to her.

He could have wept. She had ditched him. There she was, strolling up with Firth to have a nice convivial and expensive dinner at the Reef Hotel. They would stroll back afterwards, and she would be holding his arm, and when they reached her bungalow, what then?

If David Firth went into her bungalow, then Pat would present himself before they had got into her bed and he would destroy Firth – he would back him into a corner where he couldn't try any funny stuff, and he would smash him until he was unconscious.

Enid would be weeping and pleading for mercy, and before he left he would tell her what he thought of her. It would all be highly dramatic, and satisfactory.

He would need some booze beforehand. Scotch was out because it knocked him over too soon; he went down to one of the dockside drinking joints and bought a half-bottle of gin – he had a theory that it took him longer to get canned on gin.

He went down to the bay. He noticed that the third bungalow seemed to be occupied, the lights were on. He took up his post in the bushes, just behind Enid's bungalow, as before. After a while he saw the new visitor walk quite briskly towards the path; he carried a small bag, and he moved pretty nicely, like a runner.

Pat let him go and then made a careful circuit of the third bungalow. It was all locked up. He tried David Firth's and then Enid's. He couldn't get into any of them, unless he broke in, and that was not going to be necessary. He resumed his vigil, and the gin helped a little, at first.

Pinky Slowman entered the Reef Hotel by the service door, and a very anxious Charlie Olestead met him and took him straight into his office.

'They're both in the dining-room,' he said. 'They've nearly finished, I began to think you weren't coming, Pinky–'

'The name is John Brown.'

'Okay, okay.' Charlie looked uneasily at the small leather case Pinky had put on the desk.

'Just some sea-going gear,' said Pinky. 'Did you see to my boat?'

'It's ready,' said Charlie. 'And I've got a chart, the one you wanted.'

'Show me,' said Pinky.

Charlie took the chart out of his drawer and unrolled it on the desk, and began to explain to Pinky just what they were looking at – in particular the cliff-side dwelling and landing bay that belonged to Tim Taggart.

'You've been inside the house,' said Pinky, 'haven't you, Charlie boy?'

'A couple of times,' said Charlie. 'Just for the odd drink, I wouldn't call us friends.'

'Lucky for you,' said Pinky. 'He'd con the

pants off you any time he liked. Do me a working sketch of the inside as far as you know it.'

Charlie took out some sheets of paper from his desk, and began to sketch out the floor details.

'I remember one thing that may interest you,' he said. 'Vera Taggart can't get to sleep without some pills she uses – Tim says it would take an earthquake to wake her.'

'Good,' said Pinky.

'I wish I knew just what you're going to do,' said Charlie.

'You can come along for the ride.' Pinky grinned at him. 'You might even have to get your hands dirty.'

'You'll get on fine without me,' said Charlie.

'Go and check on those two in the dining-room.'

Charlie went off, and when he came back his anxious expression had increased.

'They've left,' he said. 'They finished and they left – not my fault, Pinky … they usually stay quite a while after their meal. They've gone.'

'So I'll squeeze what I want out of Tim Taggart with reference to this David Firth.'

'There could be nothing in it,' said Charlie.

'Tim Taggart is still the guy who put the bite on Harry Dollond for two hundred big ones, so that makes him my flavour of the month. I am going to shanghai that bastard, Charlie. I am going to take him with me down the coast and I am going to hold him until I can hand him over to Harry, which will make Harry a very happy man for a long time.'

'That sounds to me like a fairly tough assignment,' said Charlie.

'You couldn't do it,' Pinky agreed.

'Wouldn't it be easier if you went there by road? If you're going to break in, it would be simpler if you went over the wall where we checked the place over.'

'I thought of that,' said Pinky. 'Then I would need you to do the driving after I had grabbed Taggart, and we would have to get him down to the harbour, maybe, and load him aboard. You fancy doing that?'

'Not at all,' said Charlie. 'It's not my kind of thing, Pinky.'

'So we do it my way. I will enjoy sticking my heater in his guts, and he will know for sure that I will drop him over the side if he upsets me. Now I'll want some chow, have a tray sent in here, and make a packet up to see me through tomorrow, plenty of coffee with it. When I leave here I don't aim to come back this way. You're glad to hear that, Charlie boy? So you can wash your hands of the dirty work, right?'

Pinky made a brisk circuit of the desk, and

then sat in Charlie's chair, as of right. He was clearly happy at the prospect of some action before the night was over, and he made no effort to disguise his contempt for Charlie Olestead.

'I do what I can,' said Charlie sullenly, and went off to see about the food Pinky wanted, and Pinky's departure from the Reef could not come too soon for Charlie's peace of mind.

They had stopped at her verandah, he had his arm around her waist.

'This scene is familiar,' she said softly. 'We've played this one before, David.'

'I kiss you and then you go to bed alone,' he said. 'All very proper.'

'Will you be cross if that's what I want? Just that again?' She turned in his arms and pulled his head down and kissed him. 'Goodnight, darling David,' she said. 'Call for me tomorrow?'

He let her go, he waited until he saw her light go on and then he walked along the sand to his own bungalow, and he was feeling a little puzzled about her. Not because she hadn't asked him in for a night-cap and whatever might be expected to follow, but because she seemed to have changed since they had left Tim Taggart. He thought she had become subdued, and not quite so full of bounce.

Taggart was a crashing bore, and David

hoped they wouldn't have to see much of him, or his strange sister. However, to-morrow was another day. He would collect Enid early, they would swim, and they would spend all the time together.

Pat Quiney had watched their arrival, and he was disconcerted when he saw Firth go off on his own. This wasn't what should have happened. Firth should have gone in with her.

Pat sucked down some more of the gin, it made him cough and brought tears to his eyes, but he reckoned his mind was clearer. He felt sharp and ready to go. It was a goddam pity he wouldn't be able to give Firth a working over in front of Enid, as he had planned.

But he could say goodbye to Enid, he could make her ashamed of the way she had treated him...

He had reached her verandah before he discovered that his legs weren't doing what he wanted; they kept on folding under him, and he had to hold onto the railings. He giggled and then remembered this was a serious occasion. He straightened himself and hammered on her door.

She opened it and looked out and when she saw him she said, 'Pat – you shouldn't be here ... go on home...'

She tried to close the door but he shoved it back and went in. The light was on. She wore a short wrap, pale blue, held tight around her with one hand. She looked very angry.

'Are you out of your mind?' she said. 'Pat, what's got into you, bursting in here like this?'

'Now lemme tell you something,' he said solemnly, pointing a thick finger at her and swaying just a little on his feet.

'You're drunk,' she said abruptly. 'Go home, Pat, and sleep it off, this is stupid...'

'You are very beautiful and I love you,' he announced. 'You are also a bitch – you hear that?'

'Now I know you're drunk – I don't have to listen to any more of this.' She had backed away towards her bedroom and he was coming after her, his face was flushed and he had thrust his hands out in front of him, ready to grab at her. He looked wicked, insane, a stranger.

'Pat,' she pleaded, 'you don't know what you're doing, you're frightening me – is that what you've come for?'

'You're nothing but a beautiful bitch,' he repeated. 'Any man has to be a fool to fall for a woman like you – and I sure have been one goddam prize fool...'

'You're drunk,' she said. 'Please go home, Pat – this isn't any good to you, and I don't like it...'

'Now that's too bad,' he said heavily.

She had retreated to the wall by her bedroom door, but he had moved around to stop her getting into the room.

He laughed at her growing panic. He reached out and tore the wrap away from her. She wore a short pink nightdress, almost transparent, and the sight filled him with a raging lust.

She saw it in his eyes, she ducked under his arm and made a wild dash for the outside door. He caught her just before she reached it, and he bellowed his triumph.

He hooked his left arm round her neck from behind, he heaved her violently off her feet, and he used all of his drunken power to swing her round and round, while he stamped and shouted, until suddenly he felt the change in her body and it seemed to get heavier on his arm. Maybe he even heard the soft snap as her neck broke, but it meant nothing to him in his crazy state.

The fumes of neat gin were now getting at him, and he was seeing nothing too clearly. She still hung in his arms, and he decided that she must have fainted, although her eyes were open. He shook her a little, and her head wobbled against him. She didn't seem to have any muscles or bones – she wasn't the lovely woman he had held in his arms in that bedroom.

He carried her in and placed her carefully on the bed. He tried to arrange the nightdress so that she was decently covered. That had become important. He sat on the bed and waited for her to come round. He wasn't feeling too good about himself, his balance wasn't right. The edges of things were becoming blurred.

He patted her cheek. 'Come on, Enid,' he whispered. 'You're okay... I never meant to hurt you...'

There was no movement from her. Her mouth was twisted a little sideways, but she was still beautiful. He had never taken a pulse, and even when he concentrated hard he couldn't see any sign that she was breathing. He sat there by her and wept at the sadness. His stomach was rebelling and everything was out of focus.

He staggered across to the bathroom and groped for the light-switch, but he collapsed before he found it and his head collided with the top edge of the bath, leaving him unconscious on the floor in the dark.

David Firth was unable to sleep, so he put on slacks and a jersey, and had an abortive session at his typewriter, trying to marshal random ideas into something like a coherent pattern of words. He was not doing it very well. He lacked discipline, and probably talent as well. He made himself some coffee, and read for an hour – C.V. Wedgwood's classic *The King's War;* that was real writing.

He had read it before years back, and it still held his attention beyond midnight.

When he went out onto his verandah for a final sniff of fresh air he was surprised to see that Enid still had her lights on. So perhaps she also was finding sleep elusive, and she might welcome some company. He walked along the beach, and as soon as he saw that her front door was open with a light in the room inside he thought something might be out of order.

He called her name softly as he crossed the verandah. When he entered the room and saw her wrap on the floor by the wall, he was sure all was not right. He stood in the open doorway of her bedroom, and he didn't need to touch her to know that she was dead. The wide-open sightless eyes were turned up at the ceiling, and there was that waxen stillness about her features.

He stood there by her bed for long silent minutes, and there was nothing to indicate how she had died. No bottle of sleeping-pills on the bedside table. He could see no marks on her.

He touched nothing in the room, and left the light on. His watch told him it was twenty minutes after one, and he wondered how long she had been lying there. He found Pat Quiney on the floor in the bathroom, and he tried without success to get some information out of him. Even after a jug of cold water had been tipped over him, Pat Quiney remained a maudlin, semi-conscious wreck who could make no intelligible sounds. He just lay with his head against the bath, weeping spasmodically, and trying not to vomit too often.

He was going to be no use, so David locked him in the bathroom. Then he rode Enid's bicycle in the starlight along the coast path to Reef Town, and after searching about he fetched up at the police office.

He said his piece, as far as he knew it, and with commendable speed the duty patrolman roused Sergeant Halloran, and within half an hour the Sergeant had driven the official car as near to the bay as he could, and the investigation had begun.

Before the night was over, the resources of the Reef police force were to be stretched beyond breaking point, and an urgent phone call had to be made to the Lieutenant across the water in Fairhaven, because the Reef had sprouted a sudden crop of violent deaths. Reinforcements and technical assistance were needed.

ELEVEN

Charlie Olestead didn't want to go, but Pinky Slowman made him come down to the harbour with him.

'You can carry some gear,' said Pinky. 'You might even pretend you got some interest in the business – and I might still decide to make you my crew.'

'If anybody asks me tomorrow where you are,' said Charlie, 'what am I supposed to say? You only got here a few hours ago.'

'I'm an eccentric scientist,' said Pinky. 'I have a few dollars, so I come and go where and when I fancy.'

They reached Pinky's boat, on the Hotel's mooring. It looked slender and fast, and unobtrusive in black and grey and no brass or bright metal fixings.

'I saw nothing around here that could catch me if I have to open up,' said Pinky.

'Have a nice trip,' said Charlie. He refused Pinky's invitation to come aboard for a look-see – Pinky would think it was a hell of a joke if he set off with Charlie as a reluctant passenger.

'Chicken,' said Pinky. He got his engine going, Charlie cast off for him, and the boat moved out across the dark water, very quietly and tidily, threading its way through the harbour.

Pinky steered well clear of the coast, and he kept his speed down, lessening his chance of being heard or seen. He carried no lights. The weather was good and visibility very good. When he judged that he had come abreast of the Taggart inlet, he let his boat more or less float in, and made little engine noise, particularly when he had come close in under the cliffs.

He tied up alongside the *Mucky Duck*. He put on his shoulder harness under a loose anorak with special pockets to carry special tools he might need; he had a thin nylon rope wound around his middle, and he wore rubber-soled boots.

He started up the cliff zigzag, and he hoped that Charlie had been right about no guard dogs roaming round the place. He got to the top, and he squatted immobile for some minutes, considering his objective and making himself ready. Then he did a discreet patrol around the place, keeping to the soft ground and the grass.

He identified the window he wanted, according to Charlie's map it was a first-floor window on a landing, and it was partly open. There was a drainpipe running down the wall nearby. He tested the pipe, and it seemed secure enough to bear his weight, if he moved with care.

So he climbed, inch by inch, with the agility and balance of a trained gymnast, risking nothing, and listening for the warning creaks that might tell him the pipe was about to break away and drop him into the garden. He was ready for it, and it did not happen.

He was level with the window, he reached out and eased the window up. He got one elbow up over the ledge, hung there for a moment with his legs dangling, then he had levered himself into the open space.

There were no obstructions, like pots of plants by the window, or bits of furniture. He slid in and took out a thin torch. He began to identify the doors, working from Charlie's plan, and he had to hope that Charlie had got it right. There was the bathroom and that was easy because the door was open and it had the right smell.

The door on the left, nearer the front of the house, that would be the one used by sister Vera, so the one on the other side was the one he wanted.

It was all nicely carpeted, and there didn't seem to be any squeaky or loose boards. He stood outside the door in silence for a while. He heard the snores inside, that made it sure. Gently he palmed the door open and slipped inside like a quiet ghost. He followed the thin beam of his torch across the room to the bed. He checked the immediate surroundings of the bed, once again looking for possible obstacles in the furniture line. There was a sweaty male smell in the room, and there were clothes, heaped on a chair by the bed.

He switched on the bedside light, and at the same time his torch lit up the damp face of the sleeping man.

Pinky loosened his anorak and took out his automatic. The sleeper had started another snore, it got strangled in his throat, he papped his lips noisily, mumbled and became partly awake.

Pinky switched his torch off and slipped it into his anorak pocket, then he bent over the bed and slapped the sleeping man smartly across his face, and stepped back, smiling.

Taggart began to mumble something, his thick dark moustache shifted about and his sleepy eyes tried to focus on the figure by the bed. He grunted and began to lift himself up on one elbow.

'Who the hell...?' he whispered hoarsely, squinting.

'It's been a long time,' said Pinky.

'Oh my God, Pinky Slowman!' Taggart's mouth fell open.

'That's right,' said Pinky briskly. 'Now sit up nice and tidy – we got a little business to get through.'

Tim Taggart wore no pyjama jacket; his

chest was hairy and flabby and damp with sweat, he was in all an unlovely sight. And now he was also very frightened. He sat with his eyes on Pinky's gun.

'Harry is going to be very happy to see you again, whether you call yourself Taggart or Adam,' said Pinky.

Taggart swallowed, and waited. He had once seen Pinky shoot a guy in the belly and he had done it with no fuss. No big drama.

'What's with you and this English guy from London?' said Pinky. 'You trying to work something?'

Taggart's panic began to subside a little; he could keep Pinky talking while he thought of a way out of this mess.

'You trying to work a con on this David Firth?' said Pinky.

'It's a bit early yet to be sure,' said Taggart in his frankest manner. 'It may prove to be nothing but an unlucky speculation on my part–'

'Give it to me without the frills,' said Pinky. 'We don't have all that much time.'

'Well,' said Taggart, 'to be perfectly honest with you, Pinky, I don't think there's anything in it–'

'The day I believe you're honest I'll be ready for the funny-farm,' said Pinky. He waggled his gun around. 'Give, you slack-gutted bastard!'

'I thought Bastable Walker might be

thinking of a take-over here, Firth works for them.'

'So?'

Taggart shrugged. 'There may be nothing to it.'

'But you expect to con your way into lifting a slice of whatever's going,' said Pinky. 'I guessed as much.'

'Now listen, Pinky,' said Taggart, 'let's see if we can work out some friendly arrangement between us, on a business basis.'

Pinky smiled a chilling little smile. He moved closer to the bed, and his gun was pointing at Taggart's navel.

'You sure do stink,' he said. 'You're offering me a cut out of what you chiselled off Harry, and you kid yourself that will buy your way out.'

'A business deal,' said Taggart quickly.

'You always did have plenty of nerve,' said Pinky. 'Now get into your clothes and make it fast, we have a little trip to make together.'

'Where? Can't we discuss it here, Pinky?'

'Harry Dollond is going to be delighted to see you again.'

'Oh no!' said Taggart. 'We don't need to do that, Pinky – I've got cash in local banks, you can have all of it, we'll just wait until the morning...'

Now the sweat was running down Taggart's face and his hairy chest was dark and matted.

'Please, Pinky,' he begged, 'let's talk this over sensibly ... we don't have to drag Harry into this...'

On the advice of her doctor, Vera had been trying to reduce her nightly intake of Mogadon tablets. Instead of two she was trying to get a full night's sleep on one. It did not always work. She would wake and have to take another tablet.

It happened again, she was groping for the bottle on her bedside table, and she heard talking voices in Tim's room. She had left her door into the bathroom open in case she had to use it when she wasn't properly awake.

It was Tim's voice and he sounded frightened, and there was somebody with him, a man. Vera put the light on and got unsteadily out of bed. She remembered the gun she was supposed to have got rid of months ago – even the sight of it scared Tim. It was in one of the lower drawers of her dressing-table, wrapped in a silk scarf. A heavy revolver, loaded. She knew how to use it, and remembered about the safety catch.

There was shouting in Tim's room. In her long nightdress with frills around the neck, holding the gun in front of her with both hands, she did a Lady Macbeth progress through the bathroom and into the other room, she bumped against the door as she entered, and she was not altogether clear about what she saw.

There was a man with a gun turning towards her from the bed, and in the split second that she saw him she knew him from the past, and there was her brother half out of the bed with his mouth gaping in panic. So she held the revolver out in front of her and she began to shoot, and when the gun was jumping in her hands she still went on shooting in a blind frenzy.

The first bullet took the top off Pinky Slowman's head, another went clean through her brother's chest and slammed him off the bed and against the wall, which was in turn peppered with holes up to the ceiling. When the gun was empty she dropped it and covered her face and slid slowly down to the floor. Then it was all very quiet and still in the room and around the bed.

Much later she made herself go downstairs. She had trouble getting any answer on the phone from the police office, and when she finally made contact she had even more trouble in getting her message across – more dead bodies. Two, one of them her brother, and she had shot both of them.

She poured herself a glass of brandy, and went back up to her room. She swallowed half a dozen Mogadon tablets, drank the brandy and got back into her bed, ready for the big sleep to come and take over for good.

That had been their secret fear, that one day Harry Dollond would send somebody to find them, somebody like Pinky Slowman. It had happened, so nothing mattered any more, there had been little in Vera's life that she regretted leaving.

When her departure into nothingness seemed to be taking too long, she reached out and found the Mogadons, and crammed more into her mouth. They were difficult to get down, but she worked at it, and she won in the end.

Pat Quiney had been in a semi-drunken and very distressed condition when he was taken into custody. He had to walk part of the way before he could be loaded into the police car. During the short ride up to Reef Town, in spite of Sergeant Halloran's explicit injunction to watch himself, he managed to throw up over the rear seat of the car and Abie Garret who sat beside him, which did nothing to improve his standing with the police.

The Reef Town cells were primitive, seldom used and not designed to comfort the human spirit. Pat Quiney sat miserably on a wooden board and stared blankly at the opposite wall with his hands dangling between his knees. He had been telling them over and over that he had never meant to harm her – how could he because he loved her so much? Surely they must understand that – it had been just a rotten accident...

He had finally recovered enough to get down to the necessary business of making a statement, which took some time because he would repeat himself, in case they were missing the point, that he had loved her, and would rather be dead himself...

Sergeant Halloran allowed Aunt Emmie to see him, which was not strictly according to regulations. It had been a very painful occasion for both of them. Aunt Emmie announced that she would engage the best lawyer available to defend Pat. He might be a bit of a wild boy sometimes, but he was not a murderer.

He said it had been an accident, so that was what it had been, and Sergeant Halloran said he was inclined to agree with her, strictly off the record.

Before the arrival of the reinforcements from the mainland, and while it was still dark, David had a preliminary interview with Sergeant Halloran in the Police office.

'A sad business,' said the Sergeant. 'I know young Quiney, I've known him since he was in short pants – I agree with his aunt, I don't figure him as a murderer. A young man falls for a much older and more experienced woman, and the end is a tragedy. He had too much to drink, at this stage I am ready to accept his version of what happened.'

'He was in love with her,' said David. 'He thought I was going to take his place, cut him out with her – we had an altercation at my bungalow two nights ago, he was jealous and I couldn't talk him out of it.'

'I met him in the town,' said Sergeant Halloran. 'I gather you beat him, Mr Firth – he said it was a sailor down at the docks, he admitted he had been fighting over a woman, we didn't know who it was. He had been checked on a number of occasions late at night, and the assumption was that he was having an affair with a woman. Nothing unusual in that. Now she's dead and it needn't have happened. What are your plans now, Mr Firth? You won't leave the Reef without seeing me first, will you? I have some senior police officers coming over from the mainland pretty soon, and they will certainly want to talk to you. I'm sorry, but I just don't have the authority to tell you that you can leave, not yet.'

'All right,' said David. 'I'll stay put, but I can't pretend I won't be happy to leave Roker's Reef.'

'That is understandable,' said the Sergeant. 'It has not been a pleasant visit for you; we are usually a law-abiding community, Mr Firth. You have been unlucky, you are the most important witness we have, so you must remain available.' He got to his feet. 'You will be at your bungalow?'

'At your disposal,' said David. 'There is one thing while I'm here – do you think I could see Pat Quiney? I can't help feeling guilty about him – he thought he had reason to be jealous of me, and I think that was what started him off, I really would like to talk to him.'

'I doubt if he's in a fit condition to talk sense to anybody yet, but I'll see.' The Sergeant went out.

David gazed around the room, and reflected that police premises all seemed to have the same chilling air about them, a reminder that prison might not be far away.

After a while he found himself listening to a man's voice in the next room, although he couldn't make out what was being said, but it was obvious that the man was on the phone and that he was having some difficulty with the conversation. Several times David thought he heard the name of Taggart. There was a connecting door and he wondered if he could snoop a little.

He waited too long, and he was just getting up when Sergeant Halloran looked in on him.

'I'm sorry, Mr Firth, Quiney says he doesn't want to see you now or at any other time – will you see yourself out? We have another emergency...'

David hung around outside the police building, and very soon the police car came surging out from the yard. Sergeant Halloran was driving, and there was another policeman beside him. They were in too much of a hurry to notice a solitary spectator on the pavement. And David guessed that they were heading out towards the Taggart cliff-side dwelling. This would be the other emergency. He wished he could follow, but he had no transport, he knew he wouldn't sleep now. He made his way down to the harbour, any place was better than the bungalows on the bay. He found a small pile of timber in a corner of the quayside wall, where he sat and contemplated the harbour and the few ships and the scattered lights on the water, and in due course he managed to depress himself considerably about Enid Porter and, to a lesser extent, Pat Quiney.

He argued with himself that it had been through no fault of his that he had found himself tangled up in the tragedy. For himself, he had to admit that it had begun as a light-hearted romantic interlude, with a charming and sophisticated woman who happened to be on the spot when he arrived and that first sight he'd had of her wading out to swim and smiling in the sunshine would remain with him for a long time.

As a love affair between two adults who should have known the score it had never got off the ground. But the result had been that Enid's lovely body now lay in the hospital mortuary, and the helpless Pat Quiney was in a police cell.

When Vera Taggart had telephoned the police to tell them what she had just done, she had gone back upstairs again to prepare for her final rest and she had not unlocked any of the doors. Consequently Sergeant Halloran and his colleague, Abie Garrett, had been obliged to make a forced entry by smashing a window. The lights were on in the hall and upstairs. The Sergeant went first.

'I don't like this much,' he said. 'There's a bad smell about it, Abie…'

They found the two dead bodies in one bedroom, it was a messy scene, dried blood all over the bed and lots of it splashed about the wall by the bed, along with a ragged line of bullet holes.

On the carpet, by the bathroom door, there was a revolver.

'Don't touch anything,' said Halloran, instinctively lowering his voice at the sight of sudden death twice over. 'And mind where you're planting those great feet of yours, Abie, the forensic boys will want to crawl all over it…'

'Who was the guy who got his head blown off?' said Abie. 'I never seen him here before.'

'He won't come again,' said Halloran, 'that's for sure.'

Abie Garrett giggled and followed his superior through the bathroom and into the adjoining bedroom, and there they found Vera Taggart lying peacefully in her bed, and it was clear that she was now beyond recall.

Sergeant Halloran whispered an involuntary profanity as he began to walk around the bed, and he shook his head as he gazed down at the still figure.

'She claimed she shot those two in the other room,' he said softly, 'and one of them was her own brother, then she comes back up here and knocks herself off.'

'Pills and booze,' said Abie, looking at the stuff on the bedside table. 'She knew the right mixture, and she didn't intend to hang around and be put on trial.'

'She kept it neat and tidy,' said Halloran. 'This has been one hell of a night all round for Roker's Reef – two shootings, a suicide, and a possible accidental killing. We sure are going to need all the help we can raise.'

Before daylight a fast launch brought the police reinforcements over from Fairhaven, and with them there was a forensic team, and the Taggart cliff-top residence became the focus of much activity.

After a restless night during which he had little sleep, David Firth was in no mood to cook his own breakfast, so he went for a walk along the beach and away from the bay with the three bungalows. He eventually found his way up to the town and the Reef Hotel, and he went in for a late breakfast. There appeared to be more movement about the place than usual, and the waiter who brought his breakfast was more than willing to fill him in on the gory details about the Taggarts and the guy named John Brown who had only arrived on the Reef the day before. That was the big drama, that was what most of the cops were working on, and the unfortunate demise of Mrs Enid Porter had become temporarily less important.

David caught several glimpses of Charlie Olestead, who looked even more harassed than ever, dodging about and managing not to notice David in a dining-room that was now nearly empty. He was lingering over the last of his coffee when a man in a linen jacket and dark slacks looked into the room and came across to where David sat. He had an alert appearance, brisk and decisive. He held out his hand, smiled and said, 'I'm Lieutenant Morgan, may I join you Mr Firth?'

They shook hands, the Lieutenant sat. 'Coffee?' said David.

'Please.' The waiter had already moved off to the kitchen, and returned in no time at all with a fresh pot of coffee and the crockery. The Lieutenant said nothing until his coffee had been poured and the waiter had withdrawn. Then he gave David a friendly look and said, 'I understand you wish to leave Roker's Reef, Mr Firth? I have been over the statement Sergeant Halloran took from you, and at present I see no reason to detain you here any longer, we can always get in touch with you through your firm, Bastable Walker isn't exactly an obscure organisation, they will see you come back here if and when you are wanted.'

'Indeed they will,' said David. 'I imagine you must have your hands full now with Taggart business.'

'Did you know them?' asked the Lieutenant.

'Not really,' said David. 'I met both of them for the first and only time yesterday, they were old friends of Enid Porter's, we had lunch at their house on the cliffs... I thought they were an odd couple.'

'Yes,' said the Lieutenant. 'There is a lot to come out yet. John Brown, for instance – it will be interesting to discover what he was doing in the Taggart house just in time to get most of his head blown off – and he also had a gun in his hand when it happened, but he didn't get a chance to use it. If he was an eminent conchologist then I must be the President of the USA. I think we will find that his name isn't John Brown and that he has a record, Taggart's past will also be worth checking. Roker's Reef may not always be the tranquil little resort that some folk would like to think it is.'

'I won't give you any argument over that,' said David. 'Tranquil is not the word I'd use for Roker's Reef.'

'Perhaps you picked an unlucky time to come here.' The Lieutenant sipped his coffee thoughtfully.

'There's one thing I'd like to arrange before I leave,' said David. 'I'd like to make sure Enid Porter gets a decent burial. I don't suppose there's anybody here who knows about her next of kin, she told me she had been divorced, but she never mentioned anything about her family. She was friendly with the Taggarts, but that won't be any help now.'

'You feel responsible?' said the Lieutenant.

'I do,' said David. 'She shouldn't have died like that...'

'There'll be an inquest,' said the Lieutenant. 'I suggest you liaise with Sergeant Halloran on this, he knows the place. Unless somebody arrives with a legitimate claim on her body, you can make suitable arrangements through Halloran. I know he's busy, but I'll tell him to co-operate with you.'

'Thank you,' said David.

There was a brief silence between them.

'I understand she was a beautiful woman,' said the Lieutenant, and his voice had softened. 'What a pity her life had to end like that.'

'A great pity,' said David. 'It was senseless … it wasn't meant to happen, but it did– Pat Quiney will never forget it, and neither will I.'

The Lieutenant seemed about to say something, he paused for a moment and his expression was sympathetic. He stood up and held out his hand.

'I must be about my constabulary duty,' he said.

They shook hands and David watched him move briskly through the dining-room. After a few moments David followed, and as he crossed the foyer he saw Charlie Olestead at the door of his office, and he got to the door before Charlie could shut it in his face.

Very firmly, with both hands, he ushered Charlie back into his office.

'I'm busy,' said Charlie sharply. 'Whatever you want it'll have to wait.'

'You'll make time for this,' said David.

Charlie took refuge behind his desk. He had been through a very bad morning, so far, and he did not see it improving. Sometime soon Harry Dollond would hear about Pinky Slowman, the dirt would start flying around and Charlie knew he would come in for more than his share. One thing was sure – he would be looking for a new job.

So now he shuffled some papers on his desk, shot David a harassed look and said, 'I don't have time to bother with you now – make an appointment with my secretary.'

David laughed. 'This will be no bother. When the ferry leaves today I will be on it, so you can send your lad down to pick up my luggage. I rented the bungalow for a month, and I've occupied it less than a week, so you are well in pocket. One final point: you and the late Tim Taggart seem to have had the same crazy idea, that I had come here on some high-powered piece of business in connection with Roker's Reef. You were both fooling nobody but yourselves. I came here for a vacation, nothing else. Bastable Walker would never find anything here worth a second glance, and that includes the Reef Hotel. Any questions, Charlie?'

Charlie Olestead glared at him malevolently. 'By God,' he said fervently, 'I wish I'd never set eyes on you!'

'That could be mutual,' said David, smiling pleasantly. He paused at the door and said, 'mind you keep your hands out of the till in future, you have the police on the premises.' And on that amicable note they parted.

David found Sergeant Halloran very ready to co-operate in arranging for Enid Porter to have the right kind of funeral, and David left a cheque to cover the expenses. He expected to be available in Bastable Walker's Vancouver office for the next few weeks, and Halloran promised to get in touch with him as soon as the inquest and other formalities were done.

If it was at all possible, David said he would come back to the Reef for the funeral.

He caught the ferry with just a few minutes to spare, because he had been obliged to see to his own luggage in the bungalow. Charlie had given no instructions. He had become much too involved in another session with Lieutenant Morgan, who continued to ask awkward questions about this mysterious John Brown who had arrived out of nowhere and who had contrived to get himself separated from most of his head only a few hours after arriving on the Reef. There were plenty more questions in a similar vein, and the Lieutenant was making it clear that he was not at all happy about Charlie's answers, which was adding up to a gloomy prospect for Charlie.

It was late in the afternoon when David reached the Vancouver office. The vivacious Laura Rosen met him in the corridor, and she was patently surprised, and pleased, to see him back so soon. She followed him into the room he had been using as an office, and watched him settle himself at the desk.

'You don't look very happy, David,' she said. 'What went wrong over there on the Reef? Didn't you like it?'

'It was very peaceful,' he said, 'for a brief period. Then there was a tragedy, and I stumbled into it. Have dinner with me tonight, and I'll tell you about it.'

'I'd like that,' she said. It was obvious to her that he didn't want to say any more. He looked weary and deflated, and she promised herself that she would do her best to cheer him up in the course of the evening. She thought she knew the way to comfort him.

She smiled at him from the doorway, and she was disconcerted to realise that he wasn't aware of her. It would be different after dinner. She would see to that. All things considered, she did not expect to be sleeping alone that night. And she was not disappointed.

The publishers hope that this book has given you enjoyable reading. Large Print Books are especially designed to be as easy to see and hold as possible. If you wish a complete list of our books please ask at your local library or write directly to:

Dales Large Print Books
Magna House, Long Preston,
Skipton, North Yorkshire.
BD23 4ND